HIS SECRET BABY

LUCY MCCONNELL
ANNE_MARIE MEYER

Copyright © 2020 by Lucy McConnell & Anne-Marie Meyer

All rights reserved.

No part of this book may be reproduced in any form or by any electronic or mechanical means, including information storage and retrieval systems, without written permission from the author, except for the use of brief quotations in a book review.

PROLOGUE

PENNY

I took in a deep breath as I pulled up to the gate of Evelyn Hartman's home. Evelyn was an old family friend and the grandmother of Chris Hartman—the man I'd spent my entire life trying to forget.

But I guess the last thing a person should do when trying to forget their past is live in a town where their past is around every corner. Or in the shape of their almost five-year-old daughter's face.

I shook my head as I pressed on the intercom button and explained to the person on the other end who I was and why I was here. They confirmed, and a few minutes later, I found myself standing in the open doorway of one of Mrs. Hartman's many rooms, trying to work up the courage to go inside. Thankfully, she noticed me and beckoned me in.

"Penny, dear, it's so good to see you again," she said as she smiled up at me.

"Mrs. Hartman, it's good to see you at home." I walked across the room and leaned over to accept her hug. She was delicate and smelled lightly of rose petals and Icy Hot. I'd made the mistake of mistaking her grace for frailty. This woman was anything but frail in spirit, despite having fallen and broken her hip less than a month ago.

I was used to caring for patients, I'd made it my life's work. But this job was too close to my heart and the secrets I hid there. Just being in the house made me nervous.

"Call me Evie—everyone does—and you're not the teenage girl running around with my grandson anymore. Besides, we're not in that stuffy old hospital, and I won't stand on ceremony in my own home." She waved her hand indicating her front room.

"It's been remodeled since I was here last," I said, taking note of the missing walls. No doubt to make the room more accessible for a woman getting on in years.

"That's thanks to Chris. He takes good care of me." Her face took on a look of tenderness and joy—the kind reserved for a well-loved child who had done great things in the world.

How would she feel if she knew the truth about him?

I clamped my lips shut. No one needed to know. No one would ever know if I had anything to say about it.

The updates to the space provided enough room for her wheelchair to get around the kitchen island and the floral couches. She had more mobility at home than the hospital, but she still needed help—which was where I came in. "Let's get you settled on the couch. I'm sure you'll be more comfortable there, and we can talk about what you'd like me to do while I'm here."

"Sounds good to me." Evie's stomach rumbled.

I glanced at the kitchen. There weren't any dirty dishes in the sink. I figured she didn't have the energy to make herself something to eat and clean up after. "On second thought, I'd like to familiarize myself with the kitchen while we chat. Will that work for you?"

"You're a go-getter. I like that." She allowed me to wheel her onto the tile and up to the table. She set the legal pad of paper that had been on her lap in front of her. "I have a chef who comes in and prepares meals. They're stored in the fridge so that should take some of the load off of your shoulders. I won't stop you if you have the hankering to cook though." She let out a contented sigh. "It's good to have you here, dear."

I smiled. "I'm grateful for this opportunity to work with you."

She nodded in acknowledgement before jumping in. "I've made a list here of things I'll need you to take care of."

"Can you read it off to me? It would really help me out." I busied myself in the fridge and pantry, putting together a sandwich and a warm bowl of soup. The chef knew what he was doing—it smelled divine.

Managing medications.

Shopping.

Light cleaning.

Cooking.

Help with bathing.

"Now, I don't want sponge baths like they gave in the hospital. I want the real deal with bubbles and all." I made a mental note to check the bathroom situation. If she had a fancy tub, the kind she could walk in and out of, we'd be fine. Judging by the super expensive refrigerator and stove, she'd have top-of-the-line fixtures in the bathroom too.

I set the meal in front of her, steam rising from the bowl. She leaned over and smelled it. "Better than hospital food."

"You're right." I swallowed and wiped my damp palms on my scrubs. "Is it still okay if Katie comes with me?" My heart hammered. There were two reasons I'd even thought about taking on this private care job—and letting Chris Hartman sign my paycheck.

The first was that Evie had said Katie, my four-year-old daughter, would be able to come with me. She'd said it the first time she'd offered me the job, but she hadn't said a word about it since. I clung to that promise though. Throughout my schooling and work at the hospital, my family had been spectacular about watching Katie. Right now she was at the mall with my kid sister Lottie trying on dresses for the hospital fundraiser gala.

How I wished I was the one trying on dresses with her. She and I had shopped online weeks ago, and the results hung in our closet under lock and key. Katie was super excited about the big reveal of her princess dress. I couldn't blame her; a girl's first formal was a big deal. Since my family was well-known in the community, loved to throw parties, and donated to good causes, we had a lot of formal evenings ahead of us. Normally, I'd find an excuse to stay home, but my brother, Mason, the sheriff, had saved a boy's life and was being presented with an award. That wasn't an event I could bow out of gracefully. If there was one trait we McKnights were known for, it was sticking together.

The second reason I took this job and allowed Chris Hartman to sign my paycheck, was that Chris lived all the way across the country in California, and I would never have to see him.

I willed my heart to stop hammering. "I'll drop her off at preschool before I come and then pick her up on my lunch break or while I'm running errands. She's such a good girl, and she hardly makes a bit of noise." Okay, I was stretching the truth a lot. My daughter was not the silent type. But she did love princess movies, and I was certain that educational television could keep her entertained for at least part of the time she was here.

For the rest...

I'd just have to keep her close. She'd learn how to scrub a bathtub and vacuum and dust and whatever else needed to be done.

Evie set down her pen and pinned me with a look. "If you don't bring her, I'll fire you."

"Wha-what?" My mind spun trying to keep up with what she'd just said.

Evie laughed. The sound was low in her throat and rich—it was like pouring olive oil over the troubled waters of my heart, smoothing them out. "I've been looking forward to meeting your *little munchkin* as you call her. Why didn't you bring her today?" She looked around as if Katie would jump out from behind me and yell, "Surprise!"

My shoulders lowered, and the tension between them lightened. "I wanted some time with you first."

"I'll expect her when you start." She folded her arms over her belly and sighed. "I've always wanted a house full of children. I wish Chris lived closer, but his life is in LA now, I suppose."

I turned to the sink, looking for something to keep my hands busy. Talking about Chris was going to be an occupational hazard. "I'm sure he visits when he can."

She stared down at the table, thinking.

I'd need to find a way to keep my emotions from painting across my face when it came to him. Does a woman ever really get over her first love?

Not if Lottie was any indication. She'd been in love with Jaxson ever since he'd swaggered through our front door years ago. Then he came home, and they did this whole fake-dating thing for his image and she fell for him again. The thing was, I was pretty sure he'd fallen for her too. Only neither of them would admit it to the other.

Who was I to dish out advice? I was a failure. So, I'd told her to talk to him. Which was what I should have done when I first found out about Katie. But there were reasons I couldn't. If I had to do it all over again, I'd do the exact same thing.

But, living with a secret this big was eating away at me. I constantly looked over my shoulder. And now, working for Evie, I was putting myself even closer to the truth, and it scared me to death. But I couldn't pass up this chance to be a mom and a nurse.

Even if it could mean seeing Chris again.

I'd just have to keep my heart—and our daughter—away from him.

1

CHRIS

Breathe.

I could hear Mayor Thomas' voice coming from the stage as he began to introduce me. For some ridiculous reason, butterflies were exploding inside of my stomach.

Not flying around. *Exploding.*

Which was ridiculous. I was an actor, for heaven's sake. I was used to crowds. I was used to women throwing themselves—and other things—my direction. I could walk the red carpet with ease. I could accept awards and give speeches to thousands of people.

But walking onto the stage in front of my hometown—in front of *her*—left me feeling paralyzed.

Penny McKnight was in the audience. That thought had my mouth dry and my palms sweaty. If there was one thing I remembered about the McKnight family, it was that they stuck together. No matter what.

"...Academy Award-winning actor Chris Hartman!" Mayor Thomas said, and a thunderous applause sounded.

I swallowed and pushed myself into autopilot mode. This was when having a profession that required me to fake everything came in handy. To the world, I would look happy. I would look put together and at ease even if, in reality, it was a lie.

I was none of those things.

If anything, I was more of a shell of a person than I'd ever been before.

And maybe that was one of the reasons I'd come back in the first place. I was here to make sure Gran was taken care of and to finally put an end to my regrets. I needed to face Penny once more in order to move on.

In order to marry Jacolyn.

I approached the mic, and the personality that was voted sexiest man by *Hollywood Magazine* came over me. I made jokes and had the audience eating out of my hand. Then came the award. Sheriff Mason McKnight, Penny's older brother, stepped onto the stage. He'd done an amazing thing—saved a kid's life. Next to him, I felt...well...smaller somehow. He was a hero, and I only played one in the movies. I moved away from the microphone and nodded in his direction so that he could address the audience, but he didn't.

Instead he lifted his fingers in a small, humble wave to the crowd and hurried off the stage.

An awkward feeling settled over the audience, and I upped the charm to win them over again. They laughed, at ease once more.

I stepped away from the mic to let Jaxson Jagger take over. I wasn't sure what was going on when I saw him dressed as the Hulk, but hey, I'd roll with whatever.

We were all silent as he confessed his feelings for Lottie, the youngest McKnight, and when the spotlight moved to shine on her, my stomach fell through the floor. Just beside her was Penny. I couldn't help but stare at her as everything else around me faded away.

She looked amazing in her black dress. Her hair was pulled up with curls falling gently around her face and brushing her shoulders. Her cheeks were flushed as she kept slipping her gaze from Jaxson to Lottie.

And then, for a moment, Penny flicked her gaze up to me. Her eyes, the ones I remembered so clearly in the moments before I woke up almost every morning, were as blue as ever.

My heart hammered in my chest as I held her gaze. There was some ruckus going on, and suddenly, Jaxson jumped from the stage, but I didn't care. All I wanted was to see Penny again. To look into her eyes and verify once and for all that we were over.

Realizing that the room had fallen silent, I approached the mic and turned the evening back over to Mayor Thomas. Just as I stepped back, I saw Penny grab the arm of a little girl and head toward the doors.

Not wanting to miss my moment, I strode across the stage and down the stairs.

I kept my gaze on Penny as she made a beeline for the doors. I quickened my pace, but I wasn't fast enough. They escaped the room and were out of my sight.

Urgency unlike any I'd known spurred me on. I wasn't going to lose her. My pulse pounded in my ears, louder than the applause for the mayor.

I needed to speak to her. I needed to see if the woman I'd spent my entire adult life trying to forget was indeed the woman I remembered.

She was sweet and loving. And me? I'd broken her heart. I'd left without so much as a glance over my shoulder. I had been fighting my own demons, and Penny McKnight deserved so much better than what I'd had to offer.

I knew showing up like this wasn't fair. But I couldn't seem to move on with my life. Not when the memory of our love hovered like a cloud of mist that both comforted me and obscured my vision of every other woman out there. So I'd deluded myself into thinking that, perhaps, she felt the same.

That she needed closure as much as I did.

I nearly caught up to them in the hall. The little girl looked over her shoulder at me, and like a bucket of cold water in my face, I realized she was Penny's daughter. They had the same color skin, the same big blue eyes. If moving on was a footrace, then Penny had the gold medal.

A sense of relief washed over me as I hurried to stop her from leaving. Maybe all I needed to do was look into her eyes, know she wasn't mine for the taking, and I'd be cured.

I was desperate to be cured.

Penny zeroed in on the large exit doors. I broke into a jog and called out, "Penny?"

Her name felt so familiar on my tongue that it caused my chest to squeeze. How could the heart and body be so slow to forget? Why hadn't anything about her—about our past—faded? It felt like just yesterday we were in love.

Penny stopped so quickly that the layers of her dress swirled around her legs. She was so still, I feared I'd shocked her. I moved around so I could face her. Her eyes were wide, and her lips parted as if she wanted to say something but couldn't find the brainpower to do so.

Not wanting to be an idiot just standing there, I channeled my charm and extended my hand. "Wow, it's been a long time," I said and then winced. *That* was my charm?

What a joke.

Penny blinked a few times before she pinched her lips and nodded. When she didn't respond further, I focused on the little girl who stared up at me with wide eyes. Grateful for someone else to talk to, I crouched down and met her gaze.

"Hi, there," I said.

The little girl brought her fingers to her lips, but before she could respond to me, Penny pulled her behind her skirt as if she were trying to hide her.

Which was like daggers to my chest. She didn't even want me speaking to her child. Like I was some stranger who would snatch her away. I knew I'd hurt Penny when I left, I just didn't realize how much trust I'd lost. I couldn't blame her. After all, I'd left. I was the one who had walked out on us.

It only made sense for Penny to not want me to have anything to do with her life.

I straightened and met her gaze, only to have her focus on the ground. The tension around us was so thick I could have cut it with a knife.

Gah. I was a loser. Standing here, hoping that something miraculous would happen. That somehow I would be cured from the memories we shared.

The cure didn't come. In fact, the exact opposite had happened. The wound that hadn't quite healed broke open and gushed blood. I didn't feel happy. I hurt.

"I've gotta go," Penny said as she tightened her grip on her daughter and sprinted out the door.

I parted my lips to stop her, but nothing came out. Just before the door clicked shut, I managed out a goodbye. The door thudded behind her. And then she was cut off from me.

I'm not sure how long I stood there, staring through the glass without seeing, but it wasn't until I felt an arm snake around my waist that I turned my attention back to the present.

Jacolyn peered up at me with a bored look. She wrinkled her nose and then pouted. "That was weird," she said with a heavy sigh.

I turned to face her. I didn't want to, but I was going to have to accept the fact that Penny wasn't coming back through those doors. She was gone. For good.

That had been my chance to make amends with her, and I hadn't been able to utter more than a few words. My entire body came to a screeching halt when I was around her. If my goal in coming back to Evergreen Hollow was to move on, I'd failed horribly.

After seeing Penny, the last thing I wanted to do was leave. There was unfinished business between the two of us. Seeing her solidified that.

Not wanting to have these conflicting feelings about Penny while Jackie had her arm around me, I stepped back toward the ballroom doors. That broke our contact without being too obvious.

Jackie was, according to the tabloids, perfect for me. We were both A-list stars with a poll about us every week. According to our fans, they would die and go to heaven if we took our onscreen relationship public.

And for a while I was okay with indulging my fans. Anything I did, I did for them. Besides Gran, I had no one else to live for. Why not turn over my future to the people who cheered me on and celebrated my success?

Just like in the old days, her agent and my agent got together and concocted an engagement plan. To make us more desirable, why not give the fans a real-life fairytale? Our popularity would rise, and the jobs would roll in.

I was willing to go along with it all…until I saw the articles about Lottie and Jaxson showing up next to the ones about me and Jackie. Suddenly, my past didn't feel so far away, and ghosts began to haunt me once more. Jackie and I made our way back into the ballroom.

"Chris Hartman," a loud, booming voice called from behind me. I didn't have to look to know who was speaking.

"Mr. McKnight," I said as I plastered on a smile and turned to accept his outstretched hand.

"It is good to see you, son," he said as he pulled me in and pounded on the back a few times.

I nodded as I pulled away. Then I motioned toward Jackie. "This is Jacolyn—"

"Prescott. I know. I'm not sure you'll be able to go far without running into someone who knows who she is." Mr. McKnight extended his hand, and Jackie took it.

"You can call me Jackie," she said as she offered him one of her million-dollar smiles.

Mr. McKnight's eyes widened as he leaned forward and kissed the top of her hand. Then he straightened as Mrs. McKnight approached. She raised her eyebrows as her gaze landed on their combined hands.

Mr. McKnight dropped Jackie's hand and chuckled. "This is my beautiful wife, Brenda."

Brenda smiled, and I stepped forward to pull her into a hug. "Hey, Momma McKnight," I said.

Brenda chuckled. "It's so good to see you, Chris. I think the last time we talked was…" She pulled away and glanced up at me as her words drifted off.

"I'm so sorry." I knew what she was referring to. I could only imagine what she thought of me. And honestly, if I my daughter's boyfriend had run away without saying goodbye, I'd be a lot less polite.

"Well, that's in the past, isn't it?" she said as she reached out and patted my hand.

I could feel Jackie's inquisitive stare, but I decided to ignore it. I'd never said a word about Penny or her family to anyone in Hollywood. There were some things a guy kept to himself. Except with Penny—I hadn't held anything back from her.

"So, what are you in town for?" Mr. McKnight asked as he grabbed a flute of champagne from a passing waiter.

"Are you here for your grandma?" Carter asked as he approached.

I glanced over at him and nodded. He'd filled out a little. Another feather in the McKnight cap, Carter was a doctor. Gran loved him. Said he had the best bedside manner of any doctor she'd seen—and she'd seen quite a few lately. "Yeah. I want to make sure she's situated."

Carter slipped an hors d'oeuvre into his mouth and nodded as he brushed his hands together. "She's feisty. I assisted in her surgery. When she was coming out, all she talked about was you. She's incredibly proud of you."

My chest constricted at his words. The only woman who mattered in my life—the only one who stuck around even when I was being a dork—was Gran. Her praise was highly valued.

"I'm lucky," I said.

Carter assessed me and then nodded. "I just hope you stick around for a little while. She's lonely in that big old house."

Before I could respond, someone called Carter's name, and he excused himself.

"How long are you here for?" Mr. McKnight drew my attention back to him.

"Only the weekend," Jackie piped up.

Mr. McKnight's eyebrows rose, and I shook my head. "Probably longer than that," I offered.

I heard Jackie gasp. That wasn't the deal we'd worked out. But I wasn't going to run out on Gran now that I was here and had seen first-hand the toll her surgery had taken. Besides, I needed to take my time and work through things, no matter how long it took. If I was going to go back to LA and play the doting husband role, I needed to make sure there was nothing left for me here.

"Wonderful," Mr. McKnight said as he leaned in. "Let's schedule some time to meet on the greens at the Evergreen Hollow golf course. I'd love to catch up."

I shook the hand he extended and nodded. "Of course. That sounds fun."

He chuckled as he wrapped his arm around Mrs. McKnight's waist and guided her over to another couple. As soon as they were out of earshot, Jackie rounded on me.

"How long are we going to be stuck here for?" she asked.

I glanced over at her and sighed. "I'm going to stay as long as I need to. I'm not stopping you from leaving." One of the things we prided ourselves on was being open and saying exactly what was on our mind. It saved us a lot of arguments. I liked that about her. No games. I always knew where I stood. I grabbed an hors d'oeuvre from a passing waiter. I slipped it into my mouth as determination rose up inside of my chest.

The fog that had plagued my mind began to lift. This was where I needed to be in order to fix whatever was wrong with me. If I was going to start my life over, I needed to put this chapter to bed.

I needed to forget Penny.

And the only way I was going to be able to do that was to see her. Speak to her. Be around her without feeling like I was the yin being pulled to her yang.

Even though she was most likely going to put up a fight, I would find a way to soften her heart so she'd forgive me.

I had to, or I'd be tied to her and the love we'd shared for the rest of my life.

2

PENNY

I rushed through the door of Captain Coffee, grateful for the comforting smell of ground coffee beans and the welcoming sound of chatter as people waited for a cup of joe.

Mom had Katie for the day. They had a full schedule planned, and my daughter was in good hands. Come Monday, we'd start the preschool routine. My mama heart was tight and unhappy at the thought, but Katie was more than ready to expand her social circle and start learning her ABC's.

Seeing Chris last night had shaken me, and I'd hardly slept a wink. I had bags under my eyes and a desire to crawl back between the covers and not come out until Chris was back in California.

The worst part of seeing him? He looked amazing. Every time I saw a picture of him online, I told myself it was Photoshopped and that he couldn't possibly look that good. After all, when he left, he was a scrawny eighteen-year-old—not a man who filled out a tux like a boss.

My stomach flipped just thinking about him being all dashing and sweet, bending down to talk to Katie. Of course, he'd talk to her. He always had a way with kids. They adored him like I adored chocolate eclairs.

"Morning." Tag, part owner of the coffee shop and one of my best friends, greeted me at the counter.

"Morning. I'll take the usual."

He nodded and turned to the espresso machine to get to work. Feeling the weight of the day ahead settle on my shoulders, I let out a long and sad sigh.

"That's deep." Tag added a shot of vanilla to my cup.

"I miss Brit." Brit was Tag's fiancée and probably the most levelheaded person in my life. If she were here, she would tell me what to do. She'd take me for French fries at the local diner and tell me not to worry.

"Me too." He set the to go cup on the counter, and I counted out the dollar bills. There was no need to tell me the total—I'd been in here enough that I could probably run the place if Tag ever had to go out of town. He wouldn't. That was Brit's thing. She was deployed to Syria for the next three months. I was counting down the days until her return.

I wasn't the only one. Tag and Brit, me and Chris. It had been the four of us against the world in high school. When Chris ran off to chase his dream and leave his demons behind, it was Tag and Brit who held me up. When I ran away, I ran to Brit's. She was the one who helped me figure out I was pregnant and talked me into going home and telling my parents. I was afraid they'd kill me, but she promised they wouldn't. And they hadn't. They'd welcomed Katie with so much love it had melted my rebellious and ungrateful heart.

I'd been such a toad.

And I was being a jerk right now—making Tag all sad and mopey. "She'll be home soon." I lifted the cup like I was toasting Brit. "And we'll all have a party to celebrate."

Tag folded his arms and leaned on the counter. He had two employees working this morning, and the line moved quickly without his attention. "I hear Chris is in town."

My gut dropped to the floor like I'd climbed on the world's fastest elevator and been whisked to the highest level.

"I saw him last night." I took a sip, averting my eyes. "He's a big star now. Probably won't have time for the likes of us."

"Penny." He lowered his tone. "Does he know?"

I scoffed. "No."

He stood tall. "I'd want to know."

"That's because you're one of the good guys, Tag. Not everyone is like you."

He started shaking his head.

I glared at him. There was no way he and Chris Hartman were on the same playing field, and it angered me that he thought he was. "No, really, how many guys would run their girlfriend's business while she was deployed?"

He lifted a shoulder. "All of them."

I started walking backward, making my way to the door, so I could close the conversation before it went back around to Chris. "The fact that you think that, makes you even better." I gave him a wink, and he rolled his eyes. Thankfully, another coffee-addict stepped up and drew Tag's attention. I waved and shouted a quick, "bye," as I spun around and pushed the door open to escape into the sunshine.

Despite the cheeriness of the morning, I couldn't shake off Tag's words.

I'd want to know.

They haunted me like an echo from deep within the cave of my conscience. I mentally yelled back into the cave that it didn't matter if Chris would want to know about Katie now, because he hadn't wanted to know then. He'd left me behind like an old shirt, and I wasn't about to go begging for another chance or for money or any of the other things a father should provide for his daughter. No. I had made it this far with the help of my family and the grace of God, and I could continue that way.

I was going to push Chris from my mind entirely. I nodded resolutely as I climbed into my car and slammed the driver's door. I set my coffee in the cup holder next to me and started the engine. I had ten minutes to get to Evie's, and I wasn't going to be late.

I pulled into Evie's driveway and cut the engine. Getting through security was as easy as pulling up to the gate. They had my picture and license plate on file.

There was a flower bed in the middle of the circular drive with a fountain that gurgled. Katie would love it, and I couldn't wait to bring her here. Thankfully, she obeyed my parents' rules about their swimming pool, so I shouldn't have to worry about her diving in. But, sitting out here on the large front porch would be wonderful for her and Evie.

My gait quickened as I hurried up the large front steps and over to the door. I let myself in with the code I'd been given yesterday. The house was quiet, and I steeled myself against the possibility of seeing Chris. Surely he wouldn't stay here. My mom mentioned talking to him and his girlfriend—Jackie—last night. Ugh! The woman was practically perfect in every way, from her shiny black hair all the way down to her petite toes.

She was a model turned actress who moved with grace and dignity.

I wasn't a fan.

I made my way into Evie's bedroom and found her sitting up in her medical-grade bed, waiting for me and working on a word search puzzle book. I'd noticed several of them about the house yesterday.

"There you are." She smiled as if I'd made her day just by showing up.

My heart warmed, and I let go of many of the harsh thoughts and feelings that had followed me around since seeing her grandson the night before. Chris wasn't here, and I wasn't going to see him again, so I could let my guard down. It was exhausting to hold it up for so long. I was here to help, and that made me happy. "Let's get you dressed."

We went through the process of getting her into the tub—she did have the ultra-expensive walk-in bathtub with built-in seat and jets. Her collection of bubble baths and scented salts was impressive. I dried and curled her hair while she chatted about the news she'd watched that morning, and she gave me her opinion on the state of the world.

After she was dressed and pressed, we headed into the kitchen for breakfast. I set her at the table. "What would you like to eat?"

"Oatmeal and yogurt, if you don't mind."

"I don't mind at all." I patted her shoulder and set to work. The nurse who had been there the night before had washed pans and stacked them by the sink to dry. I grabbed one to put it away, and the whole pile tipped and fell to the floor with a loud crash.

Evie's hand flew to her heart, and she cried out at the noise.

"I'm so sorry!" I exclaimed as I bent to pick up the pans.

"Grandma!" shouted a loud voice from down the hall. "Don't move!"

Chris?

I froze in place, half standing, half crouching with a cookie pan in both hands. My entire body came to a screeching halt, and I couldn't find the brainpower to get it moving again.

He wasn't supposed to be here. Evie hadn't said a word about a houseguest or her doting grandson when we'd discussed working arrangements.

The desire to protect myself must have come over me because I crouched lower to hide behind the island, my heart hammering away and my palms clammy. This was dumb. I couldn't stay here all day, and if he found me hiding it would be so much worse. I popped up just as he careened around the counter, wearing a pair of low-slung jeans and…nothing else.

Whoa! The man had abs…and pecs…and shoulders…and eyes full of shock.

"Penny?" He looked from me to his grandma sitting calmly at the table and back again.

I cleared my throat and put a cookie sheet up to block the view.

Oh that view. I would not be sleeping at all tonight with that image flashing in my brain.

"Yep." I popped the *p* just to be a little bratty.

"Grandma, are you okay?" I peeked around the pan to see him walk over to Evie and squat down so that he was at eye level. His gaze swept over his grandmother as if he needed a visual confirmation that she was okay.

"I'm fine," Evie said with a wave of her hand and an annoyed, yet proud, expression.

"I heard a crash and thought you'd fallen again."

Evie cupped his scruffy cheek. "You're so sweet to come running to my rescue, but I'm fine."

I could see his feet, poking out from under his jeans. Did feet have an attractiveness scale? I mean, was it weird that I thought they were nice looking? Tan. No calluses or dry skin. "Do you get pedicures?" I asked before I realized what I was doing. Heat burned my skin as I turned and busied myself with picking up the spilled cookware—all the while keeping the cookie pan up to shield him from my view.

He chuckled, running his hand through his blond hair as he stood back up. He shouldn't do that, it brought his arm above the pan, and I could see all his muscles working so beautifully together. "No, I don't get pedicures. This is all natural Chris Hartman."

"I keep telling him he needs to get one."

We all turned to see Jackie breeze into the kitchen. She wore a pair of loose white drawstring pants and an aquamarine blouse that fell off one of her evenly tanned shoulders. No tan lines for this girl.

I had a great tan line from playing in the pool with Katie over the summer. When I took my swimsuit off, it looked like I had a white one underneath. I inwardly groaned as I stomped on my petty thoughts before they could fully form. These people were clients, and I was here to do a job.

I set the pan on the counter and finished gathering the others, fumbling as I did so. My hands shook and my heart was still pounding away.

"Good morning—don't you look lovely," Evie said to Jackie.

"What's for breakfast? I need protein." Jackie opened the fridge.

I glanced at Evie. Had Jackie just ignored her? Evie's lips disappeared, and her eyes tightened. I gave Chris an are-you-going-to-let-her-treat-your-grandma-like-that look. To which he furrowed his brow as he studied me. Apparently, the ability to read each other's expressions had disappeared. I sighed and shot Evie an apologetic look. She smiled and shrugged.

Jacolyn shut the door and turned on Chris, her lips puckered slightly. "What time are we leaving? I can pick something up while we're out."

Chris put his hand on Evie's wheelchair. "I'm spending the day with my grandma, but you're welcome to take the car."

She sauntered up to him and ran her hand up his arm. I looked away. There were some things a woman shouldn't have to see, and this was one of them. I felt Evie's eyes on me and made myself busy. I found a small saucepan, filled it with warm water, and set it to boil.

"Brown sugar and raisins?" I asked without turning around.

"Yes, please," Evie answered.

"Ew—brown sugar. That stuff will kill you." Jackie made a gagging sound. She flipped her silky black hair over her shoulder.

"It hasn't yet," Evie said easily.

"But if you'd taken better care of your body, your leg might not have broken when you fell."

"It was my hip, honey." Evie's southern woman was coming across in her tone. She wasn't too happy with at least one of her house guests. Good. Maybe she'd kick them both out, and we could get back to the lovely day we'd been having.

"I'll get the keys for you." Chris led Jackie down the hall, his hand on the small of her back.

I stirred the oats into the boiling water and bit my tongue. "How long are they staying?" I asked as brightly as I could.

"The weekend." Evie made it sound like fooor-eeeeev-errrrr.

I giggled. When the timer went off, I poured her oatmeal and set it in front of her. She was leaning over a bit and wearing a frown. "You've missed him, haven't you?" I asked. I could see the weight of it on her shoulders.

"I wasn't happy about breaking my hip, but I was so pleased he'd come back. I love that kid. I just…" She lifted her spoon, fiddling with it instead of eating. "I feel like I've lost him. And that harpy doesn't help. Last night I overheard them coming in. She said, and I quote, *old people are gross.*"

I took her hand in mine. "Don't listen to her. She has no idea how amazing you are and the things you've accomplished in your life."

"I just wish I wasn't through accomplishing things."

"You're not. We're going to get you healed up and moving again, and you'll take the world by storm."

Evie smiled fondly. "I'm so glad you're here."

"Me too." I hopped up, leaned down to kiss her cheek, and then started on the dishes. We didn't say much, but I could practically hear the wheels spinning in her mind. She wasn't one to take things lying down—broken hip or not.

I, on the other hand, was going to do my best to make myself scarce while Chris was here. I'd limit contact and glue my lips shut if needed while his girlfriend was around. I closed my eyes and drew on my inner well for strength. That woman was…well there weren't any nice words, so I wasn't going to say what came to mind.

Having her around was short-term. I had done hard things for years; I could do the impossible and tolerate the starlet for the weekend.

What I wouldn't be able to do was forget how good Chris looked without a shirt.

That one would be with me forever.

3

CHRIS

"But I want you to come with me," Jackie whined as she wrapped her arm around my waist and pulled herself in. She was pulling out all the stops with her big begging eyes, but I wasn't having it.

If I was being honest, I wasn't having any of her being here. She'd insulted my grandmother on numerous occasions. She complained about the water pressure and the softness of the guest bed. And then, she woke me this morning with screams of joy that some guy liked her photo on her social media account.

I'd moved her all the way to the driveway and was ready to send her off in the car to eat breakfast and do some shopping. Then I could get back into the kitchen and address the feelings that were crushing my chest.

My feelings for Penny.

"You'll do great. There's a GPS, and you can set it for anything. There are good stores downtown. I'm sure you'll find something," I said as I reached down to break her hold on me.

She sniffled and pouted a bit more, which made me realize I might not be able to get her to leave. How was it possible for such an accomplished woman to be so needy?

"Or we can go back in and spend time with my grandma," I offered.

Her nose wrinkled, and she shook her head. "I'm good. Shopping will help alleviate my stress," she said as she rose up onto her tiptoes and pressed her lips to my cheek.

I nodded and half guided, half pushed her toward the driver's door. Once she was inside, I shut the door behind her, and she started the engine. I waved as she took off around the roundabout driveway and disappeared down the road.

I let out a sigh as I shoved my hands into my front pockets and lowered my head. Jackie was nice—yes—but I was beginning to think that having her here was a mistake. I was here to heal from my past, and bringing along my current girlfriend—no matter how great the publicity—wasn't helping me any.

If anything, it made me feel farther from my goal.

I paused for a moment before I turned and headed back into the house. Fifteen minutes later, I was dressed and ready to face Penny. I hurried down the stairs and into the kitchen, where I found her standing next to the oven. I glanced around the kitchen to discover she was alone.

Not sure what to do, I gathered my strength and walked in. I leaned my hip against the counter and folded my arms as I watched her move around. The fact that she hadn't told me to disappear told me that she didn't realize I was here—which made me feel like a creeper.

So I cleared my throat, which caused her to jump and whip around. When her gaze met mine, I smiled. "Where'd Grandma go?"

Penny glanced around and then turned back toward the fridge and pulled out some eggs and butter. "She was tired and needed a nap."

I nodded as I glanced around. Flour, sugar, and vanilla were laid out on the counter. "Making cookies?" Gran was known for her love of cookies. And from what I could remember, Penny was really good at making them. Especially double chocolate chip cookies.

The sound of the fridge door closing drew my attention. Penny had her gaze focused on the ground as she made her way over to the other ingredients. "I thought I'd brighten her day," she replied.

She got busy softening the butter and measuring out the ingredients. I wanted to offer to help, but I doubted she'd take it. So I settled on keeping to the background. I didn't want to leave, but I also didn't want to get in her way.

As the mixer started, Penny peeked over her shoulder at me. I offered her a soft smile, hoping it would help ease the tension between us. It might have been the exertion from making the cookies or my smile, but I swear, Penny's cheeks flushed as she dropped her gaze back to the bowl.

With her hands now quiet, I allowed my eyes to trail down her arms to her fingers. I'd been wanting to see if she had a ring or not, but I hadn't brought myself to actually look.

Maybe it was because I didn't want to know. Maybe it was because I wanted her to be single. Wanted her to have thought about me like I'd thought about her every day since I walked away.

As my gaze grazed her fingers, a sense of relief washed over me. They were bare. No ring. Which meant she was either not married or didn't wear rings to work.

Was it wrong that I was hoping for the former?

Probably.

"Have you been working for Evie long?" I asked as I moved to pull myself up onto the countertop a few feet away from her. I leaned forward so I could catch her gaze. Penny's shoulders tightened, but she didn't break her focus.

"A few days. Ever since she got out of the hospital," Penny said, her voice low.

I nodded as I dropped my gaze to the ground and studied the flooring. "I'm happy you're here. It'll make it easier to leave."

Penny stopped moving, and for a moment, I feared that I'd said something wrong. But then a few seconds later, she started gathering up the dishes and putting them into the sink.

"When are you leaving?" Penny asked.

She turned on the water and dumped soap into the stoppered sink. Did she want me to leave?

"I was originally going to stay the weekend, but I'm thinking I need to stay longer." I narrowed my gaze as I gauged her reaction.

Penny must have been a poker player in another life. Her lips pulled tight, and her gaze narrowed as she stared at the water rushing from the faucet. "She's in good hands. You don't have to stay if you don't want to," she said quickly.

I furrowed my brow. Great. This whole *come back home to help you move on* plan was off to a great start. I'd only been here a day, and yet I was being hurried to leave again.

"Do you want me to leave?" I asked before I could stop myself.

Penny turned off the faucet and moved back to the mixer. She peered inside and then reached up to turn it off. The silence that surrounded us was deafening as she paused for a moment and then removed the bowl from the mixing stand.

I stared at her, wondering if I had actually asked what I thought I'd asked. I'd felt the words leave my lips, but Penny didn't act like she'd registered what I'd said.

Or she wanted to say something but was holding herself back.

I wasn't sure which was worse.

"I guess I figured you have a life in California. Why put off the inevitable?" Penny finally said. Her voice had dropped a few octaves, and I could see the uncertainty plainly written across her face.

Me being here was really throwing her for a loop.

And I hated that.

This wasn't what we used to be like. We used to be so open, so supportive. And now? We could barely have a conversation. Penny was closed off and distant, and even though I didn't blame her, I wanted her to forgive me.

I needed her to.

I stayed quiet as I watched her scoop cookie dough onto a baking sheet. She was so meticulous as she formed the balls and situated them so they were an equal distance apart. I could only imagine the number of cookies she'd made over the years. She was a mom after all.

My thoughts turned to her daughter, and a desire to know who the dad was grew inside of me. Was she still with him?

The girl didn't look older than four, which meant he was someone she moved on from me with. A rebound? Did I know him?

Penny opened the oven and began to slide the cookie sheet into it. Before I could stop the flow of my curiosity, I asked, "So, who's Katie's dad?"

My question must have startled her because she jumped and the cookie sheet clattered in the oven. Penny's hand went to her mouth as her eyes glistened with tears.

Realizing what had happened, I hopped off the counter and ran over to her. "I'm so sorry," I murmured as I reached out and grasped her wrist. Her eyes were as wide as saucers.

I gently lowered her hand from her lips and inspected the burn. A bright pink welt had started to form. Not missing a beat, I placed my hand on her lower back and pressed, indicating that I wanted her to move forward.

She obeyed, and as soon as we got to the sink, I turned the faucet on. Cool water flowed, and I waited for a moment before guiding her hand underneath it.

I'd managed to keep my gaze focused on the task at hand, but now, standing next to Penny, feeling her body close to mine, I couldn't help but look in her direction. I took in her beauty as she stood there, studying her hand. Wisps of hair had fallen from her bun and framed her face. The outline of her profile highlighted her lips, her nose, and even her long, dark eyelashes.

Penny was a beauty when we were kids, but now she was something else entirely.

She was a woman.

My heart pounded as I swallowed and focused my attention back on her hand. "I didn't mean to startle you," I said as I pulled her hand from the water to make sure the skin hadn't broken.

When Penny didn't respond, I glanced back at her. She nodded slightly. "I know," she said.

I swallowed against the emotions that rose up inside of me. I may be going crazy, but from the tone of her voice, she didn't sound angry. Just sad.

Wanting to fix my mistake, I stepped back. "Let me get you some ice," I said, and before Penny could protest, I began searching for a plastic bag. Once I located one—ten drawers later—I filled it up with ice.

Penny had turned off the water and was gently dabbing her hand with a towel. I made my way back to her and handed her the peace offering.

She took it and placed it gingerly on her hand. Not wanting to just stand there, staring at her again, I turned and focused my attention on the oven. The cookies seemed just fine, albeit a little melty in the hot oven, so I pushed them in the rest of the way and closed the door.

I straightened and turned to see that Penny had made her way over to the barstool and settled on it. I could feel her gaze on me. It made me feel raw and open.

"How long have you been dating Jackie?" she asked.

I wiped the countertop down with a towel and then returned it to its hook. Then, desperate for a job, I plunged my hands into the soapy water in the sink and began washing dishes.

"Not long. We sort of arranged it through our agents." I kept my focus on the dishes as I continued washing, not sure why I'd confessed that much to her.

"They do those kinds of things?" she finally asked. Her voice was quiet, and that intrigued me. I glanced over my shoulder to see that she was studying me.

I nodded. "If it benefits their client, yes."

She furrowed her brow. "And that's how you want to get married? Arranged by your agent?"

I held her gaze for a moment, hoping and wishing I could be honest with her. I wanted to tell her exactly what I was feeling inside.

How lost I'd been when I walked away. How I'd replaced that feeling with work.

How I'd bought a bus ticket to come back to her a month after I left…but none of that would make a difference anymore.

After all, she'd moved on. She had a daughter, and that daughter had a father. She seemed so settled in her life here while I was disjointed and out of place.

"When you're a person who makes lots of mistakes, it's nice when someone takes the pressure off of you," I murmured under my breath, hoping that my words made sense.

Penny was quiet for a moment before she sighed. "We were kids, Chris. We were stupid and a mess."

I glanced over to see her tracing circles on the countertop. I could hear the regret in her voice and see sadness in the slump of her shoulders.

"And now? You're not a mess?" I asked. Call me crazy, but I wanted to be the only one who was still a mess. Feeling lost was not something I wanted for her.

She deserved better.

When she raised her gaze up to meet mine, I could feel her hesitation. She chewed her bottom lip as she studied me.

"I hope he's taking care of you," I said as I rinsed the last dish and grabbed the nearby dish towel.

"Who?" she asked, her eyebrows lifting.

I cleared my throat. Who did she think I was talking about? "Katie's dad."

She stared blankly at me for a moment before she blinked and nodded. "Oh, yeah. Right. Him."

I wiped the excess water off the dishes and set them on the counter. "I'd love to meet him, if you're okay with that," I said.

Penny didn't respond right away. When I glanced over my shoulder, I could see her staring at the counter again.

"The man who won Penny McKnight's heart. That's someone I need to see."

"You already know him," she whispered.

I hesitated and then turned to see Penny's cheeks were bright red. "I do?" What did that mean? "Who is he?"

Penny's eyes were everywhere but on me, and if I didn't know any better, I'd say she looked terrified.

"Penny?" I pressed.

She swallowed and uttered, "It's Tag."

4

PENNY

I bounced Katie higher onto my hip as I negotiated my way into Captain Coffee. Tag was behind the counter, and with one glance in his direction, my pounding heart slowed. I'd prayed mightily last night that he hadn't talked to Chris before I could corner him and explain. If Chris beat me to it, that would be...catastrophic.

Katie let out a whimper. She'd worked herself into a tummy ache worrying over the first day of preschool, and we'd changed her outfits more that I cared to admit—since when did she have that many different clothing options? I couldn't be mad at her. It was normal for a child to feel uncertain in the face of change, and this girl had seen her fair share of uncertainty. My family helped provide a solid foundation of love, but I wished we didn't have to live with my parents. Someday...

"Where were you last night?" I asked Tag as I shifted Katie higher on my hip and approached the counter.

"Good morning to you too." Tag grinned and handed Katie a mini cup of cocoa.

She grabbed it in her adorable pudgy hands and took a sip.

"What do you say?" I reminded her.

"Thwanks."

I smiled as I studied her. It was nice to take a break from my life and spend some time with her, even if a hundred thoughts ran laps around my mind.

If I wasn't thinking about Chris, I was stressing about the fact that Katie's preschool teacher had said her speech patterns were behind. They had a specialist coming in to evaluate all the kids. It was normal, or so I heard, but I worried that I'd done something to hold her back. Or that I hadn't done enough to help her progress. Was there ever a place of comfort for a mother?

If my mother's worry over me was any indication, then no, there was not.

"You're welcome, munchkin." Tag leaned over the counter to rub her head.

Katie scowled at him. "No. That's my squwool air."

He laughed at her indignation. "You're as pretty as a princess."

She settled back into the spot between my jaw and my collarbone. I breathed in her strawberry shampoo smell and tried to imprint the feel of her in my arms. She was growing much too fast.

A few seconds passed before reality came racing back, and I remembered exactly why I was here and what I was supposed to talk to Tag about.

"Tag, I tried to call you like ten times last night." I'd texted him too, but I didn't want to sound like too much of a nag.

He scratched the back of his neck. "Sorry 'bout that. I was videoing with Brit. She managed to get a whole evening free, and I didn't want to, well you know. I wanted every second she could give."

My heart went out to him. As much as I missed my best friend, Tag had to miss her all the more. The pain I'd felt when Chris left was harsh, but I knew it was an inevitable end. These two pined for each other. They had their whole life together and the hope of a future.

Chris and I? We only had the past.

"What's up?" he asked as the espresso machine hissed to life behind him. He nodded toward the end of the counter where we could talk in relative private.

I'd debated how much to tell him about my confession to Chris,

HIS SECRET BABY

and with Katie on my hip, the situation was a little more delicate. I couldn't just come right out and say words like *her dad* and *her father*. Katie's speech may be delayed, but her understanding was off the charts.

"So, I'm working for Evie."

"How is she?" Tag leaned on the counter. "I miss her. I should head over there one day—take her some daisies. Weren't those the flowers she had planted out front?"

I glanced up at the ceiling, asking God for a measure of patience. Tag was only being polite, but I was on a schedule. "She's doing great. She'd love flowers and a visit. You're super nice—can I please talk for a second?"

He stood up tall. "Sure."

I sucked in a breath, gearing up to unload the long story in thirty seconds or less.

Tag's eyes brightened as he caught sight of someone coming in the door behind me. It didn't matter who it was, I needed to get this out. The bell dinged and I plunged in.

"Okay, Chris is leaving this morning, but—."

"Aw, man," Chris said, and out of instinct I turned at the sound to see him make his way up to us. "You ruined my surprise," he scolded me with a big grin.

"Chris Hartwell!" Tag hurried around the counter and wrapped Chris in a bro hug, complete with a few pounds to the back.

They laughed like dorks and their hug turned into a sort of wrestling match.

Katie lifted her head and gave me a confused look.

"I don't know why they act like orangutans, munchkin." I kissed her head.

"Orang...?" Katie asked.

I sighed. "Monkeys."

Their weird boy-greeting ended, and they pulled apart. Chris laughed as he pounded Tag on the back. "I knew coming in here was a good idea." And then, as if he suddenly noticed me, he turned to give me a wink.

A wink

"Yeah, great." I smiled woodenly. "Listen, Tag, honey," I threw in the endearment as I felt my lie from yesterday hanging over my head like a neon sign. Tag furrowed his brow as he studied me, but thankfully, he didn't make a comment.

If I didn't get to Tag before Chris spilled the beans, then my cover was blown. "Can I speak to you in the back? Now." I added a smile to soften the demand.

Tag lifted his shoulders. "Sure." Ever the easygoing type, he didn't fuss. "Ginger, get this guy whatever he wants—on the house," he called to the barista with short hair and a nose ring. She lifted her chin to let him know she'd heard.

I put my hand through Tag's arm and walked close. He looked down at me like I'd grown a third eye. "Honey?" he whispered.

"Just play along," I hissed.

We made it to Brit's office, and I practically shoved him inside and shut the door behind us. "I need you to pretend to be Katie's," I put my hand over her ear and mouthed. *Father.*

Tag stared at me. "What? Why?"

"Because I told Chris you were her"—hand over the ear again—"*dad* so he'd stop asking me questions."

"Are you insane?"

"He'll never know. Brittney isn't here. He's leaving town in less than an hour. Please, Tag?" I wasn't above begging. "It's just a little white lie."

"White lie? Try not even an option for me." Tag blew out his breath as his cheeks reddened. "I can't even have kids, Penny." Pain flashed across his face and then he scrubbed it away with his hand.

"Since when?"

"Since our senior year. Remember the fence?"

My hand flew to my mouth. "Ohmygosh! I totally forgot."

"Yeah, well I'm pretty sure Chris didn't. Guys remember those moments."

"Was it…I mean, is there a chance of a miracle baby? I mean, did everything get damaged?"

"Penny!" he said aghast. "I don't want to discuss that part of my body with you."

"Well…" I'd been friends with Tag since kindergarten—he was like a brother and a best friend all rolled into one. "I'm a nurse. I can ask these things."

He shook his head and then sighed. "There's a slim chance."

"Great—we're taking it." I snapped my fingers.

"I can't. What if it gets back to Brit?"

"You said yourself, she's going on lockdown for weeks. Chris will be long gone by then, and I promise I'll tell her all about this the first chance I get. I'll take the heat."

He shook his head. "You should be more afraid of her than you are."

I laughed. "She loves me too much to hurt me."

"Debatable," he muttered.

"Besides, it's for five minutes while he's in the coffee shop. He'll leave town, and it will be over. Brit would think it was funny."

He took a deep breath, filling his chest to capacity and then letting it out like air from a balloon. "Fine."

I grinned as relief flooded my previously aching muscles. Holding in a lie was hard. I thought I'd gotten used to it with Katie, but apparently not.

We walked back out, Katie still cuddling me close. She was so quiet I was beginning to get really worried about her. Usually my girl had spunk. I checked her forehead for a fever, but she had a normal temp. I reached for Tag's hand and immediately had that *ew* feeling you get when you're fighting with your brother and your mom makes you hold hands until you say you're sorry.

Chris waited at a table, a to go cup in front of him. He glanced up, and his gaze went straight to our clasped hands that had gotten all sweaty in a matter of seconds. It was like our bodies were trying to tell us that they shouldn't be this close or something.

"So you guys"—Chris motioned for us to sit down—"got together?"

Katie sat on my lap with her arms and legs wrapped around me.

How was I ever going to make her go to school if she didn't want to? I prayed she'd be excited once we got there.

"Yep. We did." Tag bobbed his head over and over and over again.

It was all I could do not to reach out and stop his chin from moving.

"Looks like you didn't wait too long after I was gone." Chris took a sip from his cup.

The tone was light, but the words were full of accusations.

"Well, you know. When it's right." I giggled really high and much too loud. Cutting it short, I shifted in my seat. "So, your flight leaves when?"

Chris looked back and forth between the two of us. "Actually, I've decided to stay on for a bit—get back to my roots and rediscover myself, that sort of thing."

My entire body went numb at his words. He was staying?

Tag didn't seem to understand what that meant because he offered Chris a fist bump. "Yeah. We should get together and play ball."

"Just so long as you don't decide to climb a fence again." Chris pinned Tag with a stare. "That didn't turn out too well last time. Although, the doctor was wrong about the long-term effects." He lifted his cup to Katie.

"Do you have to stay?" I blurted out, attracting the attention of Tag, Chris, and about half of the other coffee-goers in one swoop. I swallowed down my embarrassment as I patted Tag's shoulder. "Thank goodness, right, d-dear?" I said, returning to the conversation before my outburst. But even then, I couldn't get the right words out. I didn't call anyone *dear*, and never in my life would I have called a lover that. Blech.

Chris lifted his eyebrows at me.

"I mean, babe." *Babe?* Ugh. What was wrong with me? I needed to get out of here before I melted from Chris's scrutiny. "Hey, b-babe, I need to get Katie to preschool, or I'm going to be late. I'll see you later?"

"Sure?" Tag sounded as unsure about seeing me as I did about everything else. I leaned over and kissed the air right next to his cheek. He cringed away just like any normal boyfriend would have done.

This was such a bad idea.

I moved to leave, and Chris coughed. "Aren't you going to say goodbye to your daughter?"

"Oh. Yeah." Tag stood up and patted Katie on the back. "Have a good day at school, munchkin." At least that wasn't forced.

She nodded solemnly with her big blue eyes full of trepidation.

"Bye." I smiled up at Tag. I'm not sure if he thought I was going to try and kiss him—I wouldn't—or if he was just really bad at physical affection, but he patted me on the top of the head.

On that awkward note..."Bye Chris," I threw over my shoulder as I hurried away from the table.

I stepped out of Captain Coffee, feeling worse than when I went in.

Chris caught up with me as I got to my car. "Are you and Tag okay, you know, as a couple?"

I fumbled with my keys. There was no way I wanted to answer that question. If I continued, I'd probably confess that I was pregnant with Tag's triplets or something. This little white lie was rapidly becoming a giant disaster. "We're fine," I said with a high-pitched giggle. Once Chris left, then we'd be fine. Tag would forgive me for all of this, and we'd laugh about it with Brit as life returned to normal with Chris in California and me here, like I'd planned.

He jammed his fingers into his hair. "It's just...that was dysfunctional."

I placed Katie in her car seat and shut the door. "Thanks for the diagnosis, Dr. Relationship. I have to go now."

"Listen, if you ever need anything..."

"I need you to stay out of my personal life." I was one second away from breaking down, and there was no way I wanted to do that with Chris as a witness.

He stepped back, both hands in the air. "Done." Then his brow furrowed. "But, uh, I'll have to be in your professional life because, like I told Tag, I'm staying for a while."

Yep. That little tidbit was repeatedly slamming into my skull at the speed of a NASCAR racer. "Thanks for the warning."

He nodded and then focused his attention back on me. His expression softened as he reached out but didn't touch me. Instead, his fingers hovered inches from my arm. "I'm happy for you," he said. He offered me his charming smile, and despite my frustration, my knees went weak.

I didn't respond, Instead, I got in my car and drove Katie to preschool. As soon as she saw her teacher, she let go of my leg and ran off. I contemplated pulling her back into the car and demanding she spend the day with me. With the emotional hurricane going on inside of me, I needed chocolate and rom-coms to drown my sorrow. But after one glance at Katie's smile, I gripped my keys and slid back into the driver's seat.

My phone chimed as I pulled out of the parking spot. Worried it was something with Evie, I paused as I swiped the screen on. It was a text from Tag asking me what the heck my plan was now.

I had no idea and didn't want to reveal that to Tag. I sent him a question mark and silenced my phone.

My life was a giant mess, and it seemed like all I could do was make it worse. What had started out as a way to protect myself was rapidly becoming an avalanche of bad decisions.

And I couldn't get rid of this nagging feeling, deep inside my mind, that told me I wasn't the only one who would get hurt at the end of all of this. The realization of what I was doing to my daughter caused my heart to squeeze.

I just needed to hold out until Chris left. If I could do this, then I could protect my daughter. And right now, that was all my brain could understand.

Katie was my number one priority.

5

CHRIS

I stood in Gran's shed, staring at the mess in front of me. Boxes were stacked floor to ceiling, and the smell of musty memories filled my nostrils. Heat pricked at my skin, and I tugged at my shirt, which felt as if it were suffocating me.

Or maybe it was the picture of Penny and Tag and their picturesque family that had me irritated.

How could she have moved on that fast? And with my best friend?

I loved the guy, but there was a bro-code and he broke it. Ex-girlfriends were off limits. Didn't he know that?

I growled as I leaned down and wiggled my fingers under a box and then squatted down to pick it up. I hadn't anticipated the weight—it felt as if Gran was storing bricks inside of it. I shuffled from the shed and out to the blazing sun.

Even though it was the official end of summer, the heat hung around with determination. It felt as if it were making one last stand today. Sweat dripped down my face as I found an empty spot of grass and lowered the box to it.

When I'd agreed to clear out the shed for Gran, the chance to exert all of my pent-up frustration sounded like a great idea. Now that I stared at the long day of work ahead of me, I began to doubt my life choices.

I released my hold on the box and stood. I grabbed the bottom of my t-shirt and wiped my brow. Movement by the house caught my eye. Jackie stomped across the flagstone patio, heading my way.

She hit the lawn, and her steps faltered, drawing out several dark curses. Her lips pinched, and her scowl deepened every time she had to stop and pull her heel free from the grass.

I sighed as I folded my arms and waited for her to approach. Bringing her here was a mistake. Going along with her moods was easy in LA. I didn't care. I mean, I cared about her as a person, but if she got upset at a waiter, I didn't mind leaving a restaurant. If she felt slighted at a reveal party, I'd take her home and have her maid draw her a bubble bath. It was only since being with Gran—and in a lot of respects, Penny—that I started to care about what I felt, what I needed, and who I was with.

Catering to Jackie's moods was not going to help me face my history. Maybe, once I cleared things up with Penny, I'd be able to go back to being the guy who didn't need so much attention. But Jackie's demands drained me and stalled my progress. There was no way I was going to be able to move on with her pouting over my shoulder.

I also needed to keep in mind my future. Whether I liked it or not, Jackie was a part of that. I wasn't ready to agree to an arranged marriage quite yet, but that didn't mean I was never going to come around to it. Bailer promised that the fastest way to the top of the A-list was becoming an official power couple. I'd seen it work enough times to know he was right.

Except there was a part of me, maybe the part that Gran had raised, that valued marriage higher than as a career bargaining chip.

Maybe it was just best to take a break for now. Jackie was miserable here, and I wasn't leaving. We could put a pin in our relationship until I figured my crap out.

I eyed Jackie as she sighed, pulled her hair up, and fanned her neck. If I could just convince her that we were better off taking a break, I'd be golden.

"How did shopping go?" I asked as I shoved my hand through my hair and smiled.

Jackie growled as she collapsed against the nearby tree and fanned herself with her hand. "Miserable. They don't have any of the stores I like." She folded her arms and jutted out her bottom lip as she turned her focus to me. "Are you happy here?" she asked.

I furrowed my brow as I studied her. My answer had to be diplomatic. "I'm visiting my grandmother, so yeah." I reached over and pulled a leaf from the nearby bush and busied myself with ripping pieces off.

Was it wrong that I was so annoyed with her? That didn't speak well to our future together. Sure, I could work with her. But *live* with her?

Jackie sighed as she glanced around. "It's so…primitive here."

I laughed. Compared to other parts of South Carolina, Evergreen Hollow was actually prestigious. But I guess once a person is used to living in LA, everything feels like Amish country.

"It's my home," I said and then stopped. I'd spoken before thinking and the words felt strange on my tongue. Did I really feel like this was my home? I knew LA wasn't, but here?

A warm feeling grew inside of my chest, but I squelched it before it could become anything. I couldn't get attached. Not when I might leave. I broke too many hearts when I left last time, and I wasn't sure if I could stomach it again.

Jackie wrinkled her nose. "I'll never understand you," she whispered as she brushed the bottom of her dress with her hands. Then she cleared her throat and peeked up at me.

I felt bad for her. It wasn't that she was horrible, this just wasn't her scene. She'd been raised by wealthy parents who doted on her, dedicating their lives to making her acting dream a reality. Even now they ran her fan club. They were good people, and I liked them, so why did marrying into her family make me feel…off-center? Looking at her now, as she struggled to cool off in the humidity, I felt guilty for dragging her here—and even more guilty for making her stay longer than I'd originally agreed.

I sighed and made my way over to her where I pressed my hand on the tree trunk behind her, looking deep into her eyes.

"You're miserable, aren't you?" I asked as I reached out and smoothed her hair that was windblown and everywhere.

Jackie pouted as she nodded and looked up at me. "I am. It's too hot, and your grandmother's house doesn't cool properly. I'm both sweaty and cold at the same time."

I smiled at her. There were moments when she wasn't so demanding. I knew, deep down, she was a good person; it was just hard to see it sometimes. Especially when she called my grandmother gross. I wasn't over *that* yet.

"Listen," I said as I cleared my throat and tipped my face toward the sky. "I need to be here. I can't just…leave." My voice trailed off as I returned my focus to her.

She studied me, and when I met her gaze, she nodded. "Okay," she said slowly as if she wasn't sure where I was going with this.

I sighed. "Maybe it'll be best for you to head back to LA, check in with that producer you've been talking to, and I'll join you once things are settled here." I offered her a smile. The last thing I needed was for her to get upset and blow up our entire positive PR image. If I was going to work this hard for my image, I needed to make sure I treaded lightly with Jackie.

She held my gaze for a moment and then nodded. "You're right. I have things I need to do." She reached out and rested her hand on my chest as she held my gaze. "You figure out what you need to here and join me when you're ready to start living your life the way you're meant to live it, Chris Hartwell."

I nodded and pushed away from the tree. Movement to the side caught my attention, and I glanced over in time to see Penny duck behind a tree. Confused, I furrowed my brow, but she didn't reappear. I began to doubt I'd even seen her.

"What about us?" Jackie asked, bringing my attention back to her. "I need to know where we stand. People will ask."

I rubbed my chin, giving her the deep-in-thought look I used on camera. "We need to take a break."

"Why?" she spread her palms across my chest. "What good will that do?"

I tipped my head slightly, as if I could see things she couldn't. "It will keep us in the hot spot." That was my agent's term for the front pages. "If there are rumors we're breaking up, it will keep us relevant."

"I don't like it. It feels vulnerable."

"Talk to your agent about it. But I bet he'll agree with me." I prayed he would agree with me.

She nodded. "I will. And if you're right, then we're officially on a break."

I grinned.

Jackie patted my hand. "I'm going to go back and then head to the airport. Shawn said he'd have a private jet on standby just in case I couldn't hack it in the backwoods." She giggled. "He knows me well."

I gave her a quick hug and a peck on the cheek. I offered to walk her up to the house, but she waved my words away. "I'll be fine. You stay. Work," she said as she motioned toward the boxes in the shed and punctuated her feelings with a wrinkle of her nose.

I shoved my hands into my front pockets as I watched her stumble back through the grass to the house and disappear inside. Now alone, I let out my breath and focused my attention on the place that I could have sworn I saw Penny duck behind.

Curiosity won out, and I went to investigate. Just as I reached the spot, I slowed, keeping my eyes peeled for Penny. I peeked behind the tree to see her crouching with her hands over her head as if she were scared an atomic bomb was about to go off.

"Penny?" I asked, unable to keep the laughter from my voice.

"Yeah—oh!" she said as she started. Her cheeks flushed as she stared up at me. Those big blue eyes. They got to me every time, and I had to shake myself to remember why I'd come over here in the first place.

"What are you doing?" I asked as I folded my arms.

"I, um..." She glanced around as if she were looking for a plausible excuse for hiding behind trees and eavesdropping on my conversation. I wasn't upset—it meant she knew I was single.

Though why I cared that she knew was not something I wanted to investigate.

Sighing, I offered her my hand. She stared at it as if I had a disease. I growled as I reached down and grabbed her hand. She was being ridiculous. After all, she was with Tag, so what would accepting my kind gesture hurt?

Absolutely nothing.

I was the one who deserved to be hurt. She'd not only found someone new moments after I'd left, but that someone was one of our best friends. I don't know why, but it stung. Like, salt-in-the-wound painful.

I didn't have any right to be angry, but I was. She should have waited. Had a mourning period. That made me sound so egotistical. But I had mourned. I was a shell of a man when I disembarked the bus in Hollywood. There was a moment there that I wanted to climb right back on and ride it all the way to Evergreen Hollow.

I even had the ticket in my wallet to prove it.

But I didn't. I went to Hollywood to prove myself. To move on from the pain of losing Mom. When I gathered the courage to return, Gran sent me the newspaper clipping of Penny's acceptance into nursing school. It was small, but the McKnights were royalty in this town so all their news was town news.

The article hadn't said a thing about a baby.

Which made sense. If she and Tag were together, there'd be no scandal, no reason to point out her pregnancy or that she'd just had a baby. Nope, just glowing praise for the oldest McKnight daughter.

The article showed me that Penny was following her dreams when I was moments away from giving up on mine. So I stayed, and once I stayed, it was hard to leave. Hence the not coming home for years.

I tugged gently on Penny's arm, and she slowly rose to her feet. Her eyes were wide as her gaze dropped down to our clasped hands. It took a moment for my brain to register that we were still touching, and a moment later, I dropped my hand like she'd burned me.

She curled her fingers into her palm as she brought her arm up and clasped it with her other hand.

"Sorry," she murmured as she glanced around. I could tell she was trying to avoid looking at me, and that just frustrated me more.

Not wanting her to get away with eavesdropping on my conversation with Jackie, I leaned forward to catch her gaze and raised my eyebrows. "For what? Sneaking up on me or pretending that you weren't here?" I folded my arms across my chest as I stared at her.

She parted her lips, and a moment passed before her shocked expression morphed into one of indifference. "I was just heading out here to help you. Evie wants us to go through the shed together. I had no idea Jackie would be here or that you would be having a conversation that I shouldn't hear." She folded her arms as she tipped her chin a little higher. "Most people have private conversations in private—not in the middle of the yard."

I studied her before I scoffed and moved to shove my hands into my front pockets. "Gran wants you out here too?"

She narrowed her eyes and then slowly nodded. "She's taking a nap and asked if I would be willing to help." Her gaze dropped behind me as she leaned to the side. "How bad is it?" Her tone had softened, which made my heart feel as if it were melting.

Her shift from defiance to softness gave me whiplash. When she was obviously trying to keep her distance from me, I felt as if I could survive. When she changed and became the exact person I'd walked away from years ago...well that did strange things to my emotions.

Things that I wasn't ready to admit.

"It's bad," I said. I was tired of all of this. Tired of keeping my distance. Tired of hurting. We'd been friends once. We'd trusted each other once. There was no rule out there that said we couldn't do that again.

Penny's laugh came out soft and timid, and my heart began to pound at the way her beautiful lips parted, exposing her perfectly straight teeth. The memory of kissing her with so much passion flooded my body, and the inexplicable urge to do it again washed over me.

I must have been staring, because a moment later, Penny peeked over at me, and her cheeks flushed as she dropped her gaze.

"She was always kind of a pack rat," Penny whispered as she tucked a few strands of loose hair behind her ear. "But she does love you. I doubt she'd gotten rid of anything you created." Penny marked the end of her statement with a sidestep around me. I followed her with my gaze as I watched her enter the shed and place her hands on her hips.

Like a magnet, I trailed after her until I stood by her side. We surveyed the work in front of us and sighed in unison. I glanced down at her to see her eyes light up as she pressed her finger to her lips. Then a giggle erupted.

"Sorry. I'm really happy to be here to help your grandma, I swear." She walked a few feet ahead and moved to pick up a box. It must have been heavier than she anticipated because it fumbled in her hands, and she attempted to straighten it out.

Without thinking, I crossed the space between us and wrapped my arms around it. It took a second for me to realize how much of my body was touching hers. The feeling of her skin next to mine sent a fire roaring in my stomach.

I wanted to look at her, I did. I wanted to see if she felt the same. If she'd ever felt the same. I was getting to the point where I was beginning to doubt that we'd ever loved each other with an equal level of passion and devotion.

Had I dreamed it all?

Was I the only one who cared?

Was that why she'd moved on to Tag so easily after I left? Because I'd loved her more?

Seeing the same fire in her gaze that raged inside of me would confirm that we shared a monumental connection. Even if she was with Tag, there would be a flicker remaining.

But then I felt guilty. I wasn't here to reignite Penny's feelings for me. I was here to put what happened between us to rest. To once and for all get over my feelings for her.

So I kept my gaze down as I lifted the box from her arms and headed out toward the patch of grass where I'd set the previous boxes. If I had to spend the day with my head down, I would.

In my solitude I could pretend that Penny didn't care about me. I could survive in the world that I'd shoved myself into for the last five years. One that said Penny didn't care for me like I cared for her.

One that forced me to move on from what we used to have.

There I was safe even if I was brokenhearted.

There I could survive.

If there was any inkling that Penny still cared for me, I would break.

And I was pretty sure this time, I wouldn't come back.

6

PENNY

My body was like one of those glass balls in science class, the kind you touch and your hair stands on end. My skin crackled and popped every time Chris came near. When he'd reached around me to grab a box, I practically exploded.

It was memory—like a muscle memory. That was all.

I wasn't *currently* attracted to him.

I was simply reliving the feelings I'd had long ago. Somehow, he'd managed to open the chest I'd locked them in, and they were flying about like witches on broomsticks wreaking havoc on my otherwise level emotions.

I was a single mom. I was used to keeping everything I felt locked away, and it angered me that Chris could wreak havoc on that determination in a single afternoon.

Thankfully, he kept his head down and worked. I followed his stoic example and did the same until we had all the boxes on the lawn. The yard looked like a poorly organized estate sale.

"You know, some of this stuff might be worth something," I said as I ran my finger along the edge of what looked like an antique dresser.

Chris scoffed as he lifted the lid off of a box next to him and looked inside. "Yes, because the playbill from the senior musical is in such high demand." He crushed the mint-green paper into a ball and basketball shot it toward the open garbage can.

He missed.

I cocked my head. "If you'd signed it—you could have sold it, easy. Fans would fight with their credit cards to own a bit of your teen years."

A protective feeling rose up inside of me at that thought. I hated it, but there was a sense of satisfaction that, no matter what, they couldn't have his memories. They belonged to me and him and nights watching fireflies while we whispered our dreams. When you're young, just having a dream brings you together, and the process of sharing them bound our hearts. We had no idea that they wouldn't last and that eventually life would pull us apart. Who knew nursing school and Hollywood were such different worlds?

We were so naive.

He dug into the box, his shoulders hunching slightly. "I'm not that important," he mumbled, and I wondered if he was talking to me or himself.

I chose to assume that he was talking to me.

I scoffed. "The Great Chris Hartman. The sexiest man alive. Hollywood's hottest up-and-coming actor…need I go on?"

His head slowly came up, and he looked at me with a rawness and a growing understanding in his eyes. "You keeping tabs on me?"

My face heated as I swallowed hard. Shoot. I didn't mean to follow his career, but when Hollywood's heartthrob came from your hometown, it was hard to get away from it.

And if I were truly honest with myself, in the beginning, in the dark moments of my life, I'd looked him up. Sometimes, when I'd get up to nurse Katie in the night, I'd Google him and see what leading lady was on his arm.

Thankfully, that was long ago. I'd evolved to a few reliable websites bookmarked on my phone. It was both torture and therapy. Seeing him find his dream validated my letting him go and my decision not to tell him about Katie. And knowing he wasn't coming back pulled at my heart until it ached too much to read another word.

"Everyone knows you made it, Chris. It's not a secret." I opened another box and found old homework folders. I lifted out the blue one, and, out of habit, flipped to the back, my fingers grazing over the CH + PM wrapped up in a heart. I'd drawn a heart just like this on every one of his folders, always wanting him to know how much I loved him.

"You can trash that," Chris said.

I snapped the folder shut hoping he hadn't caught me looking at the heart with my eyes full of memories. Good ones. We had so many good times. It wasn't always goodbyes and secrets between us. "You sure? You got an A- on your history report."

He laughed. "Maybe I should save it then. Probably the only A I got."

I shook my head. "You were smarter than you thought."

"You too." His voice was soft and tender, and it almost undid me. "Neither of us applied ourselves. We were too busy…" His voice drifted off as if the memories of our childhood slammed into his mind as they did mine.

I turned to look at him, the intensity of his voice catching me off guard. For so long, I'd told myself I was the only one hurting from what had happened between us. That I was the only one left with a swollen belly and an uncertain life. It was painful to think he felt the same as me.

And that thought gave me the courage to face him. Maybe it was the good times coming forward, overshadowing all that happened later, that gave me the courage. When our eyes met, he looked quickly away, and my heart sank.

"You figured it out though. Nursing school is no cakewalk." He went back to sorting through the clothes he'd left behind, and I found myself stepping closer to him as he dumped them in a pile next to him.

Each item of clothing held a specific memory. The blue-striped shirt was creased from movie nights with Brit and Tag and the feeling of Hot Tamales burning on my tongue. The memory of the gray hoodie on my skin from the time we danced in the rain, laughing as we kicked puddles at each other and spun with our arms out and our faces tipped up to the sky.

He was about to stuff his ugly orange polo shirt into the donation bag when I reached out and stopped him. "Do you remember this?"

He looked from where my hand was on his forearm up to my face. A solitary line of confusion appeared between his brows.

"It's from when we went to MORP." I took it and shook it out. MORP was the opposite of prom. You wore baggy clothing with rips and tears, patches if you had them, and scuffed shoes. Girls wore their hair in ponytails. Guy's didn't shave and shoved ball caps on their heads.

His eyes lit with the memory. "You squirted catchup all down my front."

"You deserved it for buying us these hideous matching shirts. I looked like a deer hunter."

He shook open the shirt to reveal the stain. It was still there, brown and splotchy.

He smiled, the one that made my knees turn to jelly, the one I used to think was only mine—until he gave it to the world on the big screen. I used to hope that he was thinking of me when he smiled like that. Then I realized how easily he pulled it out for the cameras. But now...I wondered again. Because it was so intimate, so Chris-from-the-past, so Chris-that-I'd-loved. I hadn't seen him smile at Jackie like that the whole time she was here.

Jackie.

I dropped my hand and stepped away. Chris was in a steady on-again, off-again relationship—which, if I'd overheard correctly, was off at the moment—and I had no right to think of him, of what we used to have, with any type of longing. His life was outside Evergreen Hollow.

"Penny?"

I took another step back. His voice was too familiar. With the memories flooding my mind and opening my heart, I didn't... couldn't...handle his rawness. This was the real Chris. Not the one the cameras or the gossip sites knew. This was my Chris—and I had no right to think of him that way.

"What…" He paused. "I know you're with Tag. But is there some way you and I could…I don't know. Can we be friends?"

I laced my fingers together and squeezed. "We aren't the same people we used to be. We can't just pick up where we left off."

"I know that. I just…" He kicked the open box at his feet. "I'd like to be able to talk to you without walking on eggshells. You were my best friend."

I opened my mouth but no words came out. I'm not sure I could have formed a thought let alone a word.

Talk? Talking with Chris was dangerous.

"We don't even know each other anymore," I finally managed, though it was a weak argument.

My phone rang, and I jolted for my back pocket, grateful for the interruption. A phone call would buy me a minute to think. "Hello?" It was June—Katie's teacher. Katie had fallen asleep on the beanbag chair, her cheeks flushed. She wondered if I could come get her.

My brain flipped into mom/nurse-mode. Katie didn't crash unless she was sick. Maybe all her cuddles this morning meant more than being scared for her first day. "I'll be right there." We said goodbye and hung up.

"Everything all right?"

"Katie's not feeling well. I'm going to get her, but I should be back before Evie wakes up."

"If you're not, I'll cover for you."

I made a face. I couldn't see Chris helping his gran to the bathroom any more than I could see Gran letting him.

"Thanks. I'll be quick. If not, I'll call the hospital and get another nurse here."

He lifted a shoulder. "No worries if you can't. After all, it's what friends do."

I rolled my eyes. It seemed my protests had fallen on deaf ears. "We're not friends."

He grinned. "Says you."

"Yeah, says me."

"I say we are. In fact, I say we're pretty good friends. The kind that help one another."

"Chris," I warned.

"You can stand here and argue, but Katie's waiting. Go get the munchkin."

My breath caught hearing him use Katie's nickname, and I had zero fight inside of me to stop him from pushing me toward the house. I hurried through the door, pausing only to listen at Evie's bedroom door. Her breathing was steady, and she snored with each inhale. It was a delicate noise, like a bird chirping. She'd be mortified if I pointed it out, but it was the most ladylike snore.

I rushed to the preschool and scooped up my daughter. She was slightly warm, and her cheeks were a dusty rose. She smiled sleepily at me before nodding off again.

As I headed home, I was lighter inside. Mom agreed to watch Katie, which meant I could get back to Evie's in a timely manner. Hopefully Chris had moved on from our conversation.

It seemed I didn't have a choice about being Chris's friend. Which was kind of nice. Because I would have told myself not to do it. And I would have stuck to my guns.

The only trouble I had with this new friendship was that I'd never been able to keep things from Chris—I'd never wanted to. But I had one very big thing to keep safe, and the only way to do that was to keep my secret.

If he got close, I'd have to quit.

My eyes darted to the rearview mirror, where I could see Katie sleeping peacefully.

Katie came first, and what my heart called out for had to come second.

Chris may be here now, saying he wants to be friends. But he would leave, and I couldn't risk him breaking my daughter's heart like he'd broken mine.

I needed to protect Katie.

7

CHRIS

I was pretty sure I'd scared Penny off. After our conversation in the shed, I feared that I'd gone too fast—skipping steps of forgiveness and conversations that should have happened. Truth was, I was the kind of guy that goes for what he wants. I was like that as a kid, and it only got worse the older I got.

After all, you didn't become Hollywood's hottest actor by staying quiet.

Penny came back without Katie. A stab of disappointment hit me in the chest.

Penny's daughter was so adorable, and kids were fun. Gran was disappointed too, which made me feel even worse for being away for so long. She'd ordered a DVD of the latest princess movie to watch with Katie. Penny assured her that there would be many afternoons of movies and cuddles to come. She kept her focus on the prescription bottles she was organizing as she talked. Gran looked back and forth between the two of us and frowned.

I excused myself for a trip to the gym, but my workout was half-hearted. I just wanted to be home, so I rushed back.

Time passed as we came to a new level of normal.

Each time I bumped into Penny, throughout the week after

declaring us friends, she avoided my gaze. Her lips remained pinched and her focus steadfastly elsewhere. There was nothing that I could do or say that would pull her attention away from her job. And from what I knew of Penny, that was her signal that she'd been pushed too far.

I knew I should back away, but I couldn't. Not after what we'd shared. Her memories seemed as fresh and raw as my own. I'd even gathered up all the clothes that she had pointed out and shoved them into the bottom drawer of my dresser. I wasn't sure why—I just knew I wasn't ready to get rid of them. Did that mean I wasn't ready to move on from her? Or, was it a way of closing that chapter of my life?

I didn't know. What I did know was that I wanted to explore this friendship, and I had to find a way to get past Penny's walls.

The weekend arrived. I woke up and dressed. I headed downstairs to find another woman with Gran. They were both in the kitchen—the new nurse was making breakfast, and Gran looked miserable.

After saying hello to the new nurse, I pulled out the chair next to Gran and sat down. I wanted to ask where Penny was, but I didn't want to seem too eager. The last thing I needed was for Gran to sense my longing for Penny's company and to have her either tell me I was stupid for feeling that way…or worse, love the idea and give me false hope.

"Morning," I said as I leaned over the table and gave her a kiss on her cheek.

Gran startled and turned, but when she saw me, a smile broke out. "Well if it isn't my favorite grandson," she said as she reached out and patted my hand.

I smiled at her and then nodded toward the new nurse. There was a night nurse who came in. She dozed in the front room, getting up if Gran needed something. But for most of the day, Penny was the one who filled this place with her genuine goodness. "There's new blood?"

Gran's smile dropped as she sighed. "It's Penny's weekend off." She studied me as she mouthed, "I miss Penny."

I understood that sentiment completely. When Penny was in a room, it lit up. She had a happy way of going about her tasks, and she engaged Gran in conversation as she worked. Her productive energy and caring nature made this place feel more like a home.

The desire to learn where Penny was overcame me, so I stretched out on the chair and pulled my phone from my pocket. A few seconds later, I had Instagram up on my screen, and I selected Lottie's account.

From what I could tell, Penny had no social media presence. And trust me, I'd looked. Everywhere.

When I hadn't found anything, I'd settled on following Lottie. I weeded through the photos of her with friends—and, more currently, Jaxson—and was able to pick up on bits and pieces of Penny's life.

As I scrolled, a new photo posted. Lottie was standing in the middle of a park with Katie next to her. In the background, I could see the silhouette of Penny. She had her arms crossed and an annoyed expression on her face, and her finger was raised as if she were scolding Lottie. The caption was something about spending time with her niece.

I wanted to see Penny, and I decided I wasn't going to fight it. I'd been pushing down so many feelings when it came to that woman that I was tired of doing it.

I wanted to act.

"What do you think about getting some fresh air today?" I asked as I rested my elbow on the table and smiled at Gran.

Her eyebrows went up as she leaned in. "What did you have in mind?"

I tapped my fingers on the tabletop. "I was thinking about a trip to the park."

The new nurse straightened and turned to us. I could see her refusal in her expression, so I hurried to add, "We're in need of a grandmother-grandson day. How about I take you?"

Gran clasped her hands. "I love that idea. Hurry and grab my sweater. It's in my room in my closet." It was sweltering outside, but she would complain of the cold anyway.

"Ma'am, I have to protest. It would be better for you to stay indoors."

Gran waved her concern away and spoke to me. "Here, I'll come with you in case you can't find it," Gran said as she wheeled after me.

I wrapped my hands around the chair's handles and began pushing her. Gran turned around and gave me a wide smile.

"That's why you're my favorite grandson," she said as she winked.

I leaned close to her ear. "I'm your only grandson," I whispered.

Fifteen minutes later, I pulled into the second parking lot of the day.

"I still don't understand what you didn't like about Lincoln Park. They have a lovely duck pond."

Yes, they did. But they didn't have Penny. "The sidewalks are uneven. I would be worried about bouncing you around too much in your chair. It's not an ATV."

"I'm not that fragile," she huffed.

"You broke your hip."

"Are you ever going to let me live that down?" She scowled, but her eyes twinkled with joy. She loved sparring.

"This park is perfect." I motioned toward the path ahead of us, with smooth seams and no hills.

From where I sat, I could see Penny's strawberry blonde hair blowing in the wind. I turned off the engine and climbed out, excitement coursing through my veins.

After I removed her wheelchair, I helped Gran out and settled her in her seat. She took a deep breath. "This was a genius idea," she said as she reached around and patted my hand.

I felt a tad bad for using my grandmother as an excuse to see Penny, but then the memory of Gran's depression at the kitchen table filled my mind, and that feeling dissipated. She needed a dose of Penny's brightness too.

We were two lonely people looking for the one person who made us happy. And that one person happened to be the same person. That is what I call a win-win.

Just as I crossed the parking lot, a voice called out my name. I paused and turned to see Penny's confused expression as she approached, her lips parted.

Her cheeks were flushed—probably from the heat or exertion, but I was going to allow myself to think it was because of me—and her hair was tousled from the breeze. She wore shorts and an off-the-shoulder shirt, and she looked…amazing.

"Penny?" Gran asked as she shielded her eyes with her hand. Then she bent to the side so she could look up at me. "Did you know Penny was going to be here?"

I gave her a mischievous smile and then shook my head. "I'm just as shocked as you are."

Gran narrowed her eyes. I could see the disbelief in her gaze. "Right."

"What are you doing here?" Penny's voice grew louder as she approached.

My entire body became aware of her presence. I could sense where she was without even looking.

When I finally gathered enough courage to look up, I found her crouching in front of Gran with a worried expression.

"You should be in bed," she said in a stern, nurse-like manner.

Gran reached out and patted her cheek. "If I only listened to doctors, I would have died years ago." Penny's lips parted as if she were moments from reprimanding my grandmother, but Gran was too quick. "Isn't fresh air good for the body?"

Penny narrowed her eyes. "Yes."

"And sunshine? I remember something about vitamin D. Don't I need that?"

Penny sighed. I could see her resign herself to letting Gran have her way. "Yes."

Gran reached forward and grasped Penny's hand. "Then it's settled."

Penny studied her and then sighed. "Fine. But the minute something happens that I don't like, Chris is loading you back into the car, and you are heading home."

Gran chuckled. "Deal. Now, where is this munchkin of yours?"

I glanced over at Penny, and for a moment, I saw a flash of fear rush across her face. I furrowed my brow, but before I could process what it meant, it disappeared.

"She's saying goodbye to Lottie. I'll go get her."

"Wonderful."

I watched as Penny passed by. Her hands were clasped in front of her, and she was worrying her lip. It was strange, her reaction. I thought she would be excited to introduce her daughter to a woman who had been such a big part of her life.

Before I said anything, I wheeled Gran over to the bench and helped her sit down. Gran didn't want Katie to be scared of her chair, so she had me fold the wheelchair and set it next to a nearby tree.

I sat down next to her and wrapped my arm around her shoulders. "It's weird, huh?" I asked as I allowed my gaze to travel over to where Penny, Lottie, and Katie chatted.

Gran glanced over at me. "What?"

I shrugged. "That Tag and Penny got together and had a kid." A surge of jealousy coursed through me. I'd always figured Penny and I would get married. That she would have my children, not my best friend's. After all, that was what we talked about all the summer nights when she was wrapped up in my arms.

Sure, I'd left. But did she have to pick my best friend?

"Tag?" Gran asked, a bit of disbelief in her voice.

Confused by her response, I peeked down at her. "Yeah. Tag." I leaned forward to see that her eyebrows were sandwiched together as she stared at Penny.

"I thought he was engaged to that coffee shop owner. B...B-something. The one that's in the military."

"Brit?" Now I was confused.

"That's right. Brit. Last I heard they're planning on getting married when she gets back." Gran turned to look up at me. "But I might be wrong. I mean, she's been gone for a while. Maybe Penny snuck in there?"

I focused my gaze back on Penny, who had leaned forward and

pulled Lottie into a hug. In a few moments, she was going to head this direction. And suddenly, I didn't want her to. I wanted to continue this conversation with Gran.

After all, if what she was saying was true, it meant one of two things were happening.

One, Penny betrayed her best friend by taking her fiancé while she was overseas. But, from what I knew of Penny and Brit's relationship, I couldn't see that happening.

Or two, Penny had lied to me. Tag wasn't her fiancé, and even more, he wasn't Katie's dad. Which left me wondering, why did she lie? Was she embarrassed?

I couldn't see that being the reason.

And then a thought began to tug at the back of my mind. One that I didn't want to acknowledge no matter how insistent it seemed. And if I were honest, it was breaking my heart.

Penny didn't trust me. Whatever her story was, she didn't think she could tell me it. I had broken any chance we could have to be true friends. I had once been her confidant. I was the one she told everything to.

The loss of her trust hit me harder than any lie she could have told me.

It hurt. Physically and emotionally.

Our past was something she was never going to be able to get over no matter how much I wished it were different.

I'd lost her.

For good.

8

PENNY

"Thanks for coming," Tag said as he blew out his breath.

I smiled up at him, giving him a slight shoulder shrug. Considering what he'd done for me and Katie, going present shopping with him was miniscule. He'd texted me this morning, wanting help picking up something special for Brit's birthday in two months, and I quickly agreed. With international shipping being the way it was, we had to shop early.

It was super sweet that he was thoughtful enough to consider all of that for Brit. She'd found a good man, found him early, and treated him right. They were made for each other. If I didn't love Brit as much as I did, I'd jealously hate her for finding her man when I was seriously lacking in that department.

"It's the least I could do." I grinned. "After, you know, all that you've done for us." I glanced down at Katie. I kept a tight hold on her hand. I couldn't flat out say, "After you pretended to be Katie's dad," in front of her.

"Have you seen him lately?" Tag asked.

"Every day." I let out a breath. Evie and Katie got along famously. Katie entertained her with tea parties and stories of *Tristoff* and Sven. My munchkin had a thing for the cartoon reindeer king.

"Is it getting easier?"

"In some ways." My heart still caught the first time I saw him each morning, but it didn't break into palpitations every time. If he happened to touch me, though, my breath would hitch. I couldn't seem to get a handle on that.

"I want to wide the weapard." Katie pointed to the large cat on the small carousel.

"After we pick out a bracelet for Auntie Brit. Okay?" Brit wasn't technically my sister, but she was close. And Katie saw her often enough that the Auntie label had attached naturally to her name. I steered our group into a leather store.

Tag grinned. "When you said bracelet, I was worried." He fingered the black leather braid with a blank silver tag. "But this is genius."

I grinned. "She'd hate something sparkly." I lifted a cuff that was dark brown, an inch and a half wide, and secured with heavy snaps.

He nodded.

"And you can have any of these personalized." I pointed out.

There were several examples above the display. Tag plucked at his lower lip as he thought.

"Aw, you guys are a sight. A family out for a shopping trip," Chris said from behind us.

My hands shook, and I knocked over a stand, spilling the contents across the top of the display case. Tag scrambled to save it, but it was no use. My face flamed. "Chris," I whispered in shock. Had he said *family*?

My first instinct was to correct him, but I managed to chop that thought off before it grew too big to keep inside. As far as he was aware, Tag and I *were* a family. A nice happy little family out for some shopping.

I couldn't stop shaking as I attempted to clean up my mess. The clerk hurried over. "I'll take care of it." He handed me a wooden smile like one would hand out a ten percent off coupon. I took the hint and backed away from the mess, feeling like a reindeer with too many antlers in a store full of breakables.

Tag and I turned around to face Chris at the same time, our hands behind our back. My head hung like I'd been brought before the principal.

Though taller and broader in the chest than mortal men, Chris did his best to blend in with the other shoppers by wearing a baggy jean jacket and a ball cap to hide his honey-blond hair. He'd shaved, which actually made him look different because his Hollywood-self usually sported scruff.

I couldn't help but stare at his fresh cheeks. They didn't look as soft as they had been in high school. They looked…manly. And his jaw was chiseled. Of course I knew all this, but it hit me afresh standing there in the mall surrounded by the scent of leather.

Katie scooped down and picked up a black leather accessory with silver accents and several smaller braids twisting around a flat cuff. It was particularly pretty. "Dis one for Bwit." She held it up to Tag.

"That's perfect munchkin," Tag said as he reached down and tousled her hair.

"For who?" Chris leaned down, tipping his head to the side to hear her better.

"Bwit."

He glanced up at me to interpret. My throat tightened. "For Brittney. She's overseas and her birthday is coming up." I took the bracelet and handed it to Tag. "Thank you, sweetie."

Chris took a calculating look between me and Tag. For a moment, I feared that our cover story had been blown open somehow. That the truth of the situation was standing between us and holding a giant sign that said *I LIED*.

Tag examined the gift closely. "I think this is the one." He gently bopped Katie on the nose.

"Wait, you guys are still friends with Brit?" Chris pointed between me and Tag. I could only imagine the thoughts he had about me being the world's worst best friend for stealing Brit's boyfriend or some other such nonsense.

My gut churned with guilt. I would never betray the woman who had stood by my side when my world fell apart. This little white lie was eating away at me. If I wasn't so sure Brit would have my back, I'd have fessed up right then. Even though she never agreed with my desire to forget my past—mostly Chris—she understood why I was cautious and protective.

She'd seen the tears, the sobs, the body-wracking loneliness I'd suffered after Chris left. And, I would do anything for her—in a heartbeat.

"Of course," I managed to get out.

"I'll take this one." Tag handed the gift to the clerk.

Chris raised an eyebrow. "Don't you mean *we'll* take that one?"

What was his deal? He acted like a dog on the scent. If he was trying to sniff out the truth, he'd have his nose to the ground for the rest of his life. This was one skeleton that was going to stay in the closet.

Tag lifted a shoulder like it wasn't a big deal for him to buy a gift for his ex-girlfriend while shopping with the mother of his child. The clerk listened intently to our small talk as he rang Tag up. The store was empty, so he must be glad that something interesting had walked in.

I didn't like being this kind of interesting. I reached down and lifted Katie, settling her on my hip, so we could leave faster than we'd come in. "That's it for us. We should get going."

"Wait." Chris stopped me with a hand on my arm. Heat pooled in my belly at his touch, and my tongue lost all ability to move. It just sat there in my mouth. I was sure I was moments away from sweat rolling down my face with how warm my body got from his touch. "I want to congratulate you two properly. Let me take you out to dinner." He glanced down to his hand on my arm and yanked it away as if he'd been burned.

I glanced at Tag who had a hard no etched into the set of his jaw. Tag was a go with the flow kind of guy. He hated confrontation and playing games. This charade was rapidly getting more complicated than what he'd agreed to.

"Um..." I hedged.

"I won't take no for an answer." Chris slapped Tag on the arm. "Tomorrow night, Bella e Buona, six o'clock."

Before either Tag or I could come up with an excuse, Chris pulled his cap lower over his eyes and was gone. I watched through the glass storefront as he walked away with long strides.

"I think he's onto us," Tag said, his voice low as he accepted the receipt from the clerk.

The clerk's eyes widened as he glanced between me and Tag. I could see the curiosity in his gaze, which only fueled my desire to get out of here.

I tightened my hold on Katie. "Maybe. But he'll be gone soon and then everything can get back to normal."

Tag threw his arm over my shoulder as we left. It was such a brotherly move that I drew comfort from it. "We'll get through this, Pen."

I sniffed as tears stung my eyes. I didn't deserve a friend as true as Tag.

"I can't help but think you should tell him, though." He glanced down at Katie in my arms. "As a guy, I'd want to know. And Chris isn't the type to run away from a responsibility."

His words ate away at the momentarily good feelings that he'd brought out. "That's exactly why I can't tell him. He'd insist on being a part of her life. But for how long? It'd seem perfect now, but his life—his career—they'll get in the way." I took in a deep, reserved breath, gaining confidence in my words and my decision. "He'd abandon her eventually, and I can't let that happen. It's better for everyone for him to just go. If he's not part of her life, things will be better." I shrugged as if that was all I needed to say.

Tag paused, considering me. "Penny, I know you're scared, but—"

"I have good reason to be," I interjected. When Tag raised his eyebrows, I stared him down.

Our battle only lasted a moment before he nodded, allowing my argument to stand. Even though I could see in his gaze that he didn't agree with me, he wasn't going to push me further.

See, great friend, great guy. I sighed, hating that I was being like this. "Brit's so lucky to have you," I offered, hoping it would help alleviate the stress that surrounded us.

He half smiled. "It's the other way around."

I sighed. Maybe one day I'd meet a man who thought of me like that. But that man wasn't Chris. We had our chance, and we let it go. Neither of us fought for our relationship, and we'd both lost.

The best thing we could do was to walk away. To move on with our lives like what we had in the past was just that, the past. He could move on with Jackie, or whomever he found to be his wife and the mother of his children.

I could stay in Evergreen Hollow with Katie and raise her on my own. She was all that I needed. Men complicated things. They hurt you. They left.

Even though I was happy for my best friends and their successful relationship, I knew that would never happen for me. And I was okay with that.

I was okay with being perpetually single, depending only on myself. I would never disappoint myself, and I would never leave.

Staying single was safe, and that's what I needed to be.

Safe.

I allowed the sadness of that thought to rush through me—I felt it, felt all of it, for the first time. The washing, cleansing feeling took my anger right along with it, and I was left feeling stronger. More capable of moving forward. Whatever that looked like.

I had no idea what my future held or how my life would play out. And, yeah, that was scary. But it wasn't as scary as it could have been, because I was stronger for what I'd been through.

I could let the past break me or build me.

So far, I'd been running from it, scared that it would break me. From here on out, I was going to face the past, face Chris, and dare them to try.

9

CHRIS

Standing in the bathroom, staring at my unruly hair, I got the sudden urge to shave my entire head.

I was having a manly panic attack.

Everything I did—everything I wore—looked ridiculous. Who was I kidding? Penny and Tag knew the real me. Whatever facade I put up, they would see through it. If I was trying to look high-powered and confident? They wouldn't buy it.

It didn't help that I'd spent the entire day racking my brain as to how I would confront them. What does a person wear when they are about to call out their best friend and ex-girlfriend on a lie? What shirt was the best at saying, "come clean, scoundrels"?

Even with all the auditions I'd had, none of them came close to helping me feel prepared for this evening's conversation.

It surprised me how dedicated they both were to keeping this lie alive. I'd given them the opportunity to come clean, and yet neither seemed willing to budge.

Which hurt.

It wasn't like I couldn't handle the truth. Whatever happened after I left five years ago, whomever Katie's dad was, I wasn't going to judge.

There was a point in our relationship where I was Penny's confidant. Where I was the person she turned to when she needed advice or a shoulder to cry on. I was used to being the person she ran to, not from.

Being on the outside hurt more than I could have imagined. It wasn't until I watched her lie to my face that I realized how far we'd drifted apart. Suddenly, the thought of us ever being friends again was rapidly slipping through my fingers. I wasn't going to be able to fix what had happened between us.

Ever.

Growling, I grabbed my suit coat and threw it on. I flipped off the light and pulled open the door. I needed to get this evening over with before I drove myself crazy with self-doubt.

The entire drive to the restaurant, I went over what I was going to say, and I finally settled on the truth. I'd tell them what I suspected, and I'd wait to see what they said. If they held to the lie even after I confronted them, then I could walk away with the confidence that I'd done what I could to make things right.

The problem wasn't going to be with me but with them.

It would hurt, but I was sure that I would find the strength to move on. To go back to Hollywood and start the rest of my life. Eventually, Penny would fade from my mind. I'd find a wife and have a truckload of kids. All the while, knowing I'd done what I could to make amends. To make up for the mistakes that I made as an inexperienced and hurting kid. There wasn't a person on the earth that didn't screw up, and I was no exception.

At least I could live knowing I'd done what I could to remedy those mistakes. Even if the one person I wanted to make things better with, refused to let me.

I pulled open the door to the restaurant. My nose filled with the smell of garlic bread and marinara. My stomach growled as I approached the hostess stand. A woman with black hair and rainbow-colored glasses glanced up at me.

The restaurant was quaint. The walls were a deep red with all sorts of images from the Italian countryside. Even though it felt small town, the food was anything but. It took months to get a reservation—but not for Chris Hartwell. One call, and they had a private room for me when I wanted it.

And I'm not going to lie, it made me feel good. Ever since I got here, it seemed like I was rejected left and right. To have someone recognize me—even if it was the hostess at a restaurant—made me feel good. Right now, my ego was so beaten down that I needed a boost. As pathetic as that sounded.

"Good evening, Mr. Hartwell. We have your table ready," the hostess said as she stepped away from the stand and extended her hand. I followed her to the back of the restaurant, where a table had been set up in a secluded room. Candles were lit and resting in silver candlesticks.

I nodded as I pulled out a chair and sat. The hostess took my drink order and left. I leaned back in my chair as I tipped my head back. My thoughts were reeling. Where were Tag and Penny? Were they coming?

Would they ride together?

My heart began to race as I thought about Tag helping Penny out of the car. Linking arms and looking at each other—even if it was fake—like they loved each other.

Whatever joke they were playing on me, it wasn't fair. I'd been their friend once. We'd been honest to each other in the past. Why was now any different?

As I felt myself spiral, I cleared my throat and opened my eyes. I straightened in my chair and gathered my confidence. I could handle whatever they threw at me. I was Chris freaking Hartwell. I could do this.

The server came back with my drink, and my phone chimed.

I pulled it from my suit coat and glanced down at the screen. It was a text from Tag.

Sorry, man. I can't make it.

I stared at the words. He was bailing? Why? Did that mean Penny wasn't going to come?

I growled as I tossed my phone onto the table. This was getting ridiculous.

"Right through here, ma'am." the hostess' voice broke through my thoughts.

Confused, I glanced over to see the drapes part. The room faded away as Penny entered. She wore a dark-red, fitted dress. Her hair was pulled back, exposing her collarbone and the length of her neck.

Her eyes widened as her gaze landed on me. It might have been the lighting or my imagination, but I swear her cheeks flushed. She paused as she ran her gaze over me and then around the room.

"Sadly, you have just me," I said with a shrug and then moved to focus on the empty plate in front of me. I took a certain satisfaction from the fact that she hadn't come with Tag. That maybe they really weren't this couple that they claimed to be.

That maybe I could still read her.

The hostess led her to the table and pulled out the chair across from me. Once Penny sat, she informed us that our waitress would be in soon to take our order, and then she left us alone.

Silence engulfed the room as I sat there, trying hard not to stare at Penny. It wasn't fair for her to look this beautiful. I had come here to pull the truth from her, but one look at the beauty sitting across from me, her eyes holding vulnerability, and I lost the driving need to pound the truth out of her with a confrontation.

It didn't help that I couldn't form a coherent sentence to save my life.

Even when I thought about the speech I'd rehearsed on my way here, the harsh words had left my tongue feeling like lead in my mouth. I wanted Penny to talk to me like she used to, to share willingly, not be yanked into a confessional with breadsticks. I was pretty sure attacking her with my assumptions wasn't the way to get us back to a place void of awkwardness.

I needed to make a decision right here, right now. Did I want a future with Penny, or did I want to be right? I couldn't have both. Not when Penny was as skittish as she was.

She was a delicate flower that I needed to coax open. If manhandled, she'd crumble. And that was the last thing I wanted.

My answer floated to the front of my mind as I reached out and fiddled with the silverware. I wanted a relationship with Penny more than I wanted to catch her in a lie. If she wasn't telling me the truth, there was a reason, and I was okay with waiting to find out what that reason was.

She'd tell me eventually. I had to have faith that there were parts of our past that lingered in the back of her mind. Moments we shared that were good, that meant something to her.

I needed to find a way to bring those moments to the forefront of her mind. Then she'd tell me. She'd open up once again.

I had to have faith.

"How do you like being a nurse?" I asked as I reached out and grabbed my glass to take a drink.

Penny's eyes widened as she stared at me. Then she glanced to the empty chair at the table. "Tag's not coming?"

I furrowed my brow. How did she not know? "He texted and said he couldn't come. He didn't tell you?"

She parted her lips and paused before she snorted and waved me away. "Oh right. I forgot." Then she took a drink while tipping her gaze away from me. "He told me."

I eyed her, the realization of her dishonesty rising up inside of me again, but I muscled it down. "Happens to all of us."

Sadie Rivas walked through the curtains, wearing a black shirt and pants. I recognized her from the award ceremony I'd been asked to emcee where Penny's brother was awarded a medal for saving Sadie's son's life.

Her eyes widened as she stared at me, and then her gaze lingered on Penny.

The awkwardness between her and Mason at the ceremony wasn't lost on me. I knew a little of their history. Mason had served with her husband when he passed away. Ever since then, it seemed as if she hated Mason. Handing the award over to him had been more awkward than onscreen kisses. History zinged between them like a pinball, but neither acknowledged it. I'd had to wade through it to maintain the lighthearted feel of a charity auction.

"Name's Sadie, and I'll be taking your order tonight," she said as she pulled a pad of paper from her apron and readied her pen.

Avoiding the obvious turned out to be the special tonight.

I peeked up at Penny as she studied Sadie for a moment. Penny finally said, "You look good, Sadie. I like what you've done with your hair."

Sadie reached up like she was going to brush her hand over her light-colored tips. I couldn't remember what the look was called, but it was all the craze. "Thanks." Her eyes darted between the two of us, and she managed a nervous smile.

"What's your favorite dish?" Penny asked.

I felt for Sadie. All she wanted was to get away from us, and Penny wasn't letting it happen. After a few compliments on her taste and understanding of the menu, Sadie started to loosen up, and I had a newfound respect for Penny. She'd helped Sadie feel confident and safe.

If only I could do the same for her.

We placed our order, and Sadie tucked my menu under her arm before she left.

Alone once more, I steepled my fingers and rested my elbows on the table as I leaned forward. Penny looked everywhere but at me, her chattiness from moments ago gone. Her clamped lips were driving me insane.

I wanted to get her to talk to me. It was the only way I was going to be able to break down this wall that she'd built up around herself. I racked my brain for topics we could talk about. I doubted Hollywood was of any interest to her. Especially since my going there was the reason we broke up in the first place.

I wasn't sure what her hobbies were, and when I mentioned nursing, she slid right past it. The only other thing I could think of was Katie.

"Katie's adorable. She's how old now?" I asked as I unfolded my napkin and set it on my lap.

"Who?" Penny asked quickly. Her eyes were so wide that she reminded me of a deer in headlights.

"Katie," I said slowly. If she sidestepped this topic, I'd resort to talking about the weather.

Penny pinched her lips together as she dropped her gaze and fiddled with her plate. "She's four."

Well, that was a start.

"Is she in what…first grade?"

Penny chuckled. "Preschool. Some days, she acts like she's fifteen. That girl is giving me gray hair." Her voice was quiet and caring, and her expression was gentle. The love she had for Katie emanated from her.

It was the look she used to give me; one of complete and utter acceptance and adoration.

My heart ached as I studied the woman that I'd loved—that I still loved. She was beautiful, soft, and vulnerable. Every part of her called out to me. I wanted to wrap her in my arms and take away all the stress that pulled her down.

I wanted to be the guy she once believed I was. More than I'd ever wanted anything in this world.

"She's lucky to have you as a mom. You'll do right by her."

Penny stopped moving and a few seconds ticked by. I furrowed my brow, wondering if I'd said something wrong. A sniffle sounded from across the table. Confused, I leaned forward to see tears glistening in Penny's eyes.

"I'm sorry," I said as I hurried to pull my napkin from my lap. I rounded the table and kneeled next to her.

She must have not noticed because her gaze stayed focused forward.

"Penny," I whispered as I reached out with the napkin and ever so gently wiped a tear that had slipped down her cheek.

She startled, turning her gaze to me. I held it as if holding a glass sculpture, careful and with all my attention, hoping she could see everything I couldn't say. I wanted her to know that what I'd said was true. I'd always known she was going to be an incredible mother.

I'd always known she was going to make it.

I'd always loved her.

And I'd never forgotten her.

Whatever she was keeping from me, she could tell me. She could trust me.

I wanted—no, I needed her to know that. Words failed me. If only I could show her, then things would change.

I leaned forward ever so slightly, stilling my gaze as I held hers.

Penny didn't falter as she stared at me. Time stood still as we stayed there, studying each other.

"Excuse me," she whispered. In slow motion, she turned away from me and stood. She didn't look back as she hurried from the room, disappearing from sight.

I sat back on my heels. I couldn't tear my gaze away from where Penny had sat. Something had happened between us. Something that I knew still existed and, up until now, had doubted Penny still felt.

But that moment, that electricity, that zap through us, told me all I needed to know.

Despite whatever was happening with Tag and Penny and the ridiculous lie they'd spun, one thing was for sure.

Penny still loved me. Like I loved her.

And for the first time since coming back, I felt something I'd doubted I was capable of feeling.

Hope.

10

PENNY

I stared at myself in the bathroom mirror. The stress lines around my eyes were deeper. The tension in my lips was noticeable. The exhaustion from keeping Chris out of my life and heart was a visible weight on my shoulders, pulling them forward.

The way he looked at me, like he loved me, was too much to fight. I didn't have walls tall enough or thick enough to keep him out—because my heart was inside those walls beating against them just as hard as Chris was from the outside.

In the end, all it meant was that keeping him at arm's length bruised me inside and out.

I couldn't do it anymore.

He'd asked to be my friend, and I'd refused. The consequences for that were plain on my worried forehead.

I dabbed some cold water on my cheeks and then dried them. It was time to stop fighting so hard. I could be friends with Chris. It wouldn't kill me.

And, if I gave in a little to that voice inside who called out for him, maybe she'd find peace.

I took a deep breath and glanced around the bathroom. The marbled tiles and sleek black stalls were calm in the same way a clean bedroom was calm. There wasn't any work to do. As a single mother, I was constantly bombarded with chores, picking up toys, soothing Katie, reading to Katie, playing with Katie…there was always so much to do.

But not tonight.

Tonight, I had a free pass. Katie was with my brother Mason. I had the night off, and I needed it. A smile tugged at the corner of my lips. I straightened my back and made my way back to the table.

Chris was staring down at the table, a large to go bag sitting in the middle.

"Hey," I said low. I didn't want to startle him. Plus, I was a little embarrassed about walking out on him when things got real. I'd never run away from him before. He was always the one to leave first. This was uncharted territory, and I wasn't sure how I felt about it.

His head came up, and his eyes found mine immediately. They searched my face, and I smiled carefully.

"Do you want to leave?" he asked. "We could eat on the beach."

I closed my eyes for a brief moment, the memories of a hundred beach picnics running through my mind. If we were going to get along as friends, the beach was the perfect place to start.

"That sounds nice."

He studied me for a moment with his gaze searching mine. "Are you sure? I can take you home if you want."

I gathered my courage up inside of me and nodded. "Yes, I'm sure."

He was on his feet in a flash as he snagged the bag by the handles. "Let's go." A weight seemed to have lifted off him too.

I did a self-check, evaluating my walls and safeguards. I was doing okay.

Until he took my hand on the way out of the restaurant.

My face flooded with heat, and my whole arm tingled as if he'd plugged my fingers into a socket. He held it for a moment, and then a second later, he dropped it as if he suddenly realized what he'd just done. I kept my lips pinched together as we weaved through the tables and out the door into the warm summer night.

His touch lingered on my skin, heating it from only the memory.

How easy it had been for him to touch me. He'd held my hand so many times in the past that, for a moment, I hadn't even realized that it had been a mistake.

A mistake I wished he'd do again.

Walls. I need walls.

The waves roared in the distance, and a light breeze brushed my bare arms. I shivered, but when Chris glanced back at me, I stilled. The last thing I needed was him offering me his suit coat. I had willpower, but if I was wrapped up in something that had his scent, that held his warmth, that willpower would be as fleeting as the light from a firefly.

We walked along the path for a few minutes, ducked under a low-hanging branch, and then the stone path disappeared and my feet sunk into the soft, white sand.

"Hang on." I reached down and slipped off my shoes.

"Great idea." Chris did the same, rolling up his pant legs and tucking his socks into his shoes. He took my heels out of my hand and tucked them under the tree.

"If there's a spider in there when we come back, you're buying me new shoes. I'd never be able to wear those again," I said, trying to lighten the mood. We'd been so serious tonight that the desire to elevate it overcame me.

He chuckled, the sound was familiar and yet new. There was a depth to it that hadn't been there before. Dare I say it was a manly sound? I put the brakes on those thoughts and started toward the water.

"Wait up," he called after me.

I broke into a run and laughed over my shoulder. "First one to the water wins."

The takeout bag hit the sand, and I giggled inside as I pictured the sad state of my lasagna. I didn't care. I wasn't a mom tonight. I wasn't Nurse McKnight. I was just Penny. Free and fun. The girl who could run into the surf and not care about the laundry she'd have to do later.

My walls were heavy and exhausting. I was tired of caring so much. They would still be there in the morning. My past could haunt me tomorrow. Tonight, I was going to be free.

Chris passed me with his jaw set in determination. I'd forgotten his competitive nature. I kicked into high gear, my feet sliding in the sand, but he beat me to the water, turned around, and splashed me. I squealed as the cold drops splattered my front.

He pulled back, a look of horror on his face. I'm sure he thought he'd pushed too far and ruined everything.

But he didn't know what he was in for.

I grinned wickedly as I kicked water all over his pants and then took off up the beach, all the while laughing too hard to run very fast. My feet were coated in sand. The gritty feeling caked between my toes, but I didn't care.

In seconds, Chris's very large, very strong arm was around my middle and he'd lifted me into the air.

I kicked and pushed, gasping for breath. "Chris!" I yelled as he carried me back out into the water until it reached up to his knees.

I couldn't squirm—unless I wanted to spend the rest of the night sopping wet. Instead of flailing around, I twisted and grabbed onto him. My arms wrapped around his neck and my legs around his middle.

"Don't you dare drop me."

"I don't think I can." His laugh was muffled under my arm.

I'd pinned his arm to his side. "Back out of the water, real slow," I instructed.

He held his other arm out in surrender and began walking backward. When we were over dry ground, he used his free hand to tickle my side. I yelped and dropped, landing on my backside but no worse for wear.

Chris grinned down at me. "Where'd you learn that move?" He held out his hand to pull me up.

I patted the spot next to me, inviting him to sit instead. "I have three brothers. There comes a certain point where it becomes an if-I-go-down-I'm-taking-you-with-me thing." I shrugged. "That was the point."

He laughed as he settled down and leaned back on his arms. "I'll have to remember that one."

I copied his posture. My hem was soaked and covered in sand, and I didn't even care. That five minutes was the most fun I'd had in ages.

"What's the frown for?" Chris asked.

"I was just wondering when I became such a stick in the mud."

"You?" He gasped in shock. "You're the most spontaneous person I know. When I was going for auditions, I'd get these crazy ideas on how to play a character, and it would freak me out. But then I'd think, Penny would do it. It paid off, every time."

I bumped him with my shoulder. "I don't even know that girl anymore. I miss her."

He sighed. "Me too." His arm came across my back.

I hesitated, not sure what snuggling with Chris was going to do to my wall. I peeked up at him and saw that his jaw was set. He was ready for whatever I decided.

Exhaustion took over me as I played each scenario out in my mind. I could shift toward him—like my entire body begged me to do. Or I could pull away.

My head screamed at me to move away, but my heart? That was a different story. And right now, I wanted to listen to my heart. So, I did what the old Penny would have done, leaned into his chest.

"I miss the old me too." His voice rumbled in his rib cage, and I fought the desire to curl up against him. "Do you remember the time we snuck into the arcade and played Turbo until three in the morning?"

I buried my face in my hands and then instantly regretted it when my skin was coated with sand. I must have looked desperate because suddenly Chris's tie came into view as he began to wipe my cheeks. All I could do was stare up at him. He avoided my gaze as he continued wiping.

He finished and dropped his hand. I cleared my throat as I tried to backtrack to what we had been talking about.

I took in a deep breath. "Please don't remind me. If Katie does half the things we did…"

"She's half you, Pen. She's bound to have a wild side." He looked over at me with his eyebrows raised in an implicating manner. If anyone would know, it was him.

I moaned. *Half me and half you*, I thought. "I'm doomed."

"Nah." He shook his head. "You've been there. You can't pull a trick on a trickster. She doesn't stand a chance."

I grabbed a handful of sand and let it cascade out of my fist. "She's actually a sweetheart. I don't see the same stubbornness in her that was in me back then."

"Back then?" he teased.

I bumped him again. "Okay, still."

He searched my eyes. "You have changed—and not all for the bad."

I elbowed him. "Gee, thanks."

He rubbed his side where I'd gotten him. "You know what I mean."

I did. Because I knew Chris.

"How about some dinner?" he asked.

"Sure."

He grabbed the bag and came back, sitting in front of me this time. I tucked my legs off to the side, and he sat crisscross. We opened our containers, and the smell of marinara sauce mingled with the salty sea.

I took a deep breath before cutting my first bite.

"Whatever happened to Rob?" Chris asked as he twirled alfredo around his fork.

I swallowed. Rob was one of the guys who'd hung out with us sometimes. He and a few others were smart enough to go home before we did things like sneak into the arcade. "He works in Vegas as an Elvis impersonator."

Chris's mouth fell open. "No way."

I laughed and held up my hand as if swearing an oath. "Cross my heart."

"Huh. I would not have pictured that. What about Julie?"

Julie was Rob's high school sweetheart. "She's married to some guy she met in college. They have a couple kids and a house over on 3rd. I see her around. Helped deliver her babies."

"I can picture that." He bobbed his head as he took another bite. "Brad?"

I frowned and lowered my container to my lap. "He's in jail."

"What for?"

"Drugs. I heard he's clean though and doing an inmate college program of some sort. Mason keeps tabs on him—he feels responsible since he was the one who arrested him."

"Mason's a good guy."

"Always has been." I winked and picked up my plate. "I often wondered if that was part of the reason I rebelled so much. Mason was just so good, there was no use going that direction, I'd never catch up." I stared at my food in shock. I had never—never!—said those words out loud to anyone, and I just dropped them in a conversational tone to Chris.

I peeked at him out of the corner of my eye. He looked out over the water, thinking over my confession. What must he think of me? That I was a twit, probably.

He tipped his head. "I don't know. If you rebelled because of Mason, what was my excuse?"

"My bad influence?" I blurted out.

He laughed. "Probably."

I kicked his leg, but he only laughed harder.

"You weren't a bad influence, Penny." He set his food down and put his hands behind him again to lean back. "You were an answer to my prayers. I needed you like I needed air. I never would have made it through high school without you."

My jaw fell open. We'd been skirting around our past feelings, so for Chris to say them like that—to be so...open—it shocked me. I was pretty sure my face was as red as my dress when Chris moved to meet my gaze. He held it for a moment before he cleared his throat.

"But that was back then. We've both moved on. Right?" The tone of his voice was inviting. As if he were asking something so much more.

I reached up and brushed some strands of hair off my cheek. "Right," I said in a way that even I didn't believe.

His gaze grew cautious, and I struggled with the desire to

backtrack. We were having so much fun, and I had to go and ruin it like that. I wasn't afraid of him. Not like I had been. Really talking with Chris was good for me, good for my soul and my heart. And even though I'd spilled one secret, that didn't mean I had to give them all away.

Maybe we *could* be friends.

Our phones buzzed at the same time. "That can't be good," he said as he pulled his out.

"It's Evie," I guessed before even looking at the screen. If it had been Katie, only my phone would have gone off. Sure enough, it was the night nurse.

One text. Four words.

She's got a fever.

We both stood up, not even needing to talk about who was going or how we'd get there. It was like the connection that had allowed us to finish each other's sentences was still there, still strong, still working to bring us in sync.

I liked how comfortable it felt, like an old pair of jeans worn in all the right places.

I'd just have to watch myself. Chris was leaving. And while I could reminisce about the good times and enjoy his company, I couldn't—under any circumstances—allow my heart to fall for him again.

I'd survived him leaving once—a second time would break me.

11

PENNY

My heart pounded as I drove back to my house. I was a woman on a mission, and I wasn't going to stop until I had Katie buckled in the back and I'd pulled into Evie's driveway.

Even though the night nurse had assured me that she had it under control, my nerves were on high alert. I was going to be there all night if I had to. There was no way I was leaving Evie to anyone else.

I'd texted Mason as I climbed into the car, asking him to pack Katie a bag and to have her ready to go. He had to work tonight, and my parents were out of town. I would have had Lottie watch her, but she was with Jaxson and Liam at some formal event for their team.

Plus, I figured having Katie there might be therapeutic for Evie. She loved children with all her heart. That day Chris had taken her to the park and she'd watched the kids play had done more to lift her spirits than my homemade chocolate chip cookies ever could. I was determined to do everything I could to make sure she healed and healed quickly.

As soon as I pulled up to my parents' house, I honked. Mason must have heard, because a moment later, the front door opened and he stepped out. He had one arm hooked under a sleepy Katie and the other held her My Little Pony backpack. It looked silly draped over his massive bicep. His time in the military had filled him out, and as the sheriff, he made an imposing figure in his uniform. Just the sight of him scared half the kids in town into doing the right thing. But under all that bluff and muscle, he had a gummy bear's soft heart.

I hurried over to him, resting one hand on Katie's back. Her eyes fluttered open, and she smiled down at me.

"I'm ready for my sleepover," she whispered.

"I told her that the magic fairy is needed. She's packed her feel-better dust and everything," Mason said. His voice was deep and gruff, and I couldn't help my smile. Dainty, Mason was not, and to hear him talk like this was adorable.

Why he hadn't been snatched up was beyond me.

"Thanks, Mason," I said as I pulled open the back door and stepped out of the way so he could settle Katie in her car seat. After he buckled her in, he straightened and pulled me into a hug.

When he stepped back, his eyebrows went up as he dusted his hands. "Rolling around in a sand pit?" he asked.

I waved off his comment as I rounded the car to the driver's side. "No time to explain. I need to get to Evie," I said over my shoulder.

Mason's questions lingered, but I pushed right on past them. He may be my brother and a darn good police officer, but that didn't mean I had to have an alibi. As I drove away, I wondered what my family would think if they knew my history with Chris. Mom and Dad thought we were part of the same crowd in high school—a couple of friends in a bigger group. I'd never told them that I loved him.

I glanced at Katie dozing in the back. There were a lot of things I hadn't said.

Fifteen minutes later, I pulled into Evie's driveway and parked. I gathered a now very awake Katie from the backseat, who bounced up and down. She talked about how she was going to heal Granny Hartwell. How it was going to take *two* sprinkles of healing dust to help her get well.

I joined in on the conversation, making sure to prepare her for the fact that Evie might not be awake, but Katie didn't seem to mind.

Instead, she said, "I know, Mom." *Hello thirteen-year-old.* "Don't worry, I'll be gentle."

I slung Katie's backpack over my shoulder and followed after her as she skipped and jumped across the cracks of the driveway. When we got to the front door, I knocked softly and then opened it. I doubted anyone would mind if I let myself in.

The house was quiet. I reached down and grabbed Katie's hand. The last thing I needed was for her to wake up Evie. I was going to get her settled down in front of the TV and then head to Evie's room for an update. She could sleep on the couch for the night with a couple of blankets.

Once *Paw Patrol* was on, Katie instantly zoned out, and I was able to slip from the room and head to Evie's. Quinn, the night nurse, stood outside of the room with a perturbed expression on her face. Her arms were folded across her chest, and she kept sighing.

I gave her a sympathetic smile, but I wasn't going to back down. She was leaving, and I was taking over.

"Thanks for waiting for me to get here," I said as I lifted Evie's chart and glanced over it. Her fever had spiked, and it spiked fast.

Quinn sighed again. "I told you I had it handled. There was no reason for you and Mr. Hartwell to rush back so fast." She narrowed her eyes. "I'm a good nurse."

I nodded as I glanced up at her. "I know, I know. But I feel better about being here for this." I patted her on the shoulder. "Go home and get rested. I'll see you tomorrow?"

Quinn humphed and turned, disappearing around the corner.

I sighed as I set the chart down on the small side table next to Evie's door and then turned the handle. The room was dimly lit. Her side lamp was on, but there was a sheet covering it to lessen the brightness of the bulb. My eyes adjusted quickly, and I found Chris sitting on the edge of the bed.

He brought a cool washcloth to Evie's forehead and began to dab gently. A sound, like he was singing, drifted to my ears. I leaned in to listen.

My heart took off galloping as his words met my ears. He'd been in a band in high school. And he'd been good. If he hadn't made it as an actor, I was pretty sure he would have made it as a singer.

Chris Hartwell could not only act, but he could sing.

My knees weakened, and my body flushed. I moved closer to the bed. I wanted him to sing louder. I wanted to hear the melodious notes as they left his perfect lips.

His singing, combined with the gentle care he took as he attempted to cool down his grandmother, was making my wall crash down around me. Suddenly, the last thing I wanted was for Chris to leave. Ever.

I swallowed hard against the emotions that had risen up inside of my chest. My head grew foggy as I neared them.

Chris's gaze fell on me, and he stood suddenly as if he was a kid with his hand caught in the cookie jar. His hand hit the bowl of cold water, and it crashed to the floor, spilling water everywhere. The mom in me took over, and I hurried over to the bathroom to grab a towel.

The song cut off too, the silence bigger than us both. I wished he'd keep singing. I wished he'd sing to me again, the way he used to when we'd lie on the grass to watch the stars.

Chris must have also rushed to clean up the mess, because a moment later, we were sandwiched in the bathroom with our hands on the same towel. My arm was pressed against his chest, and I could feel the pounding of his heart.

I could feel his gaze on me as we lingered there as if our close proximity had stunted our ability to move.

"I've got this," he said as he pulled the towel gently away. "You go check on Gran." His voice was deep and meaningful, saying, *get out of here before I kiss you*, and it sent shivers across my skin.

Not wanting to speak and give away just exactly what was going on inside of me, I nodded and slipped from the bathroom. I busied myself with taking Evie's temperature as Chris cleaned up the water.

Her temp was still high, but it wasn't getting worse, which was good. Carter had texted me the dose of Ibuprofen to give her and said he would stop by later to check on her once his shift was over.

It took some coaxing, but I was able to wake up Evie and get her to take the medicine. She drank a glass of water and promptly went right back to sleep. Chris spent the time leaning against the far wall. His gaze was on me everywhere I went.

Butterflies bombarded my stomach as I worked. I wanted to know what he was thinking. Did he feel what I felt when we touched?

I shook my head as I tucked Evie's blanket in around her and set her monitor up so I could hear if she called for me or even just coughed. She seemed exhausted, so I doubted that she would wake, but if she did, there was no way I would miss it.

With everything squared away, I took in a deep breath as I turned and headed to the door. Just as I passed Chris, his hand wrapped around mine, stopping me in my tracks. I paused before I looked down to verify he had touched me again.

Chris was holding my hand. And he wasn't just holding my hand, he was *holding* my hand. As if he was drowning and desperate for me to save him.

He parted his lips to speak, but I didn't want to wake up Evie, so I pressed my forefinger to my lips and nodded to the door. I didn't pull my hand away as I led him out of the bedroom and shut Evie's door quietly behind me.

We stood there in silence for a moment. My gaze kept drifting down to Chris's hand as it remained wrapped around my own. When was he going to let go? *Was* he going to let go?

"Thank you," he whispered as he stepped closer. His warmth cascaded over me as he stood there, studying me.

I swallowed as I nodded. "It's my job. But I also love your grandmother. I want her around for a long time."

Just as the words left my lips, an ache grew inside of me so big that it took my breath away. What if Evie passed away without knowing that Katie was her great-granddaughter? What if Katie never really got to know her great-grandmother?

Was I selfish enough to keep those two away from each other?

Every self-defense mechanism I had built up inside of me went haywire. Sure, I wanted to be honest and open—even with the man standing in front of me—but could I do that?

Chris's concerned gaze filled my sight as he dipped down to study me. "Are you okay? Are you that worried?"

I swallowed as tears stung my eyes. I wanted to be honest. The weight of my secrets was stifling me. But I was worried. I was scared. And I wanted to run. He dropped my hand and rested both of his hands on my shoulders. "Go to my room and take a shower. You can wear one of my t-shirts and shorts."

I parted my lips to turn down his offer, but he shook his head and began to push me in the direction of his room. "I can handle Gran."

"But Katie's in the front room"

"I can handle her too. You go take care of you first."

I wanted to stop moving. I wanted to push past him and hide, but all my will to keep Chris away from Katie disappeared, and the only thing I could think about was standing in a hot shower and crying.

So I nodded and hurried away from him as I called, "No sugar," over my shoulder.

He waved me away as he turned and headed toward the TV room.

I had an idea of where Chris's room was, and when I opened the door, I found his sweatshirt slung on the bed as well as the smell of his cologne hovering in the air like a hummingbird. I closed the door behind me and took in a deep breath.

One shower. That was all. One short shower, and I would hurry back downstairs to pull Katie away from her father.

Even though I felt horrible that I was keeping Evie away from Katie, I knew one thing for sure: I wasn't ready for the truth to be told. Not yet anyway.

I needed time.

Just a little bit of time.

12

CHRIS

With Penny in the shower and Gran sleeping in her room, I made my way into the TV room to find Katie sitting on the couch, her eyes trained on the screen. The room was dark, and the light from the TV shined on her face.

I couldn't help the smile that emerged as I watched her. She didn't look the least bit interested in sleeping. Instead, she looked like a spring, ready to go off at any moment.

I flipped on the light, which drew her attention over to me. Her eyes widened as she pulled the blanket off her lap and stood up on the couch.

"Where's Mommy?" she asked as I found the remote and clicked the TV off.

I smiled over at her. "She's taking a shower. She asked if I could watch you until then." I folded my arms. "Do you think that's okay?"

Katie eyed me. "Do you wike Barbies?"

I laughed. "I've never played with them."

Katie paused and then jumped from the couch and padded over to her backpack. "I have some," she said but then stopped and turned to stare me down. "But you have to give them back."

I held up my hand. "I promise."

She studied me and then unzipped the big pocket. Soon Barbies, dresses, and tiny little shoes were dumped onto the ground. Katie sorted through the stuff, handing odds and ends to me.

"You can play with Lacy. She's crabby right now." She handed me a red-headed doll who was missing an arm.

"What happened?" I asked as I motioned to her missing appendage.

Katie shrugged. "She was sick, and I had to cut it off."

I stared at her and then slowly began to nod. Sounded like the daughter of a nurse and niece of a doctor.

Katie didn't hesitate to instruct me. Lacy was to wear the pink, frilly looking dress with the green high heels. I struggled and even broke a sweat trying to shove the doll's feet into the impossibly tiny shoes.

Once Lacy was dressed, it was time to style her hair. Whatever they made Barbie doll's hair out of was ridiculous. It looked silky but it knotted like barbed wire. I tried but couldn't get a brush through her hair if my life depended on it. Especially not the little plastic thing that looked like a choking hazard. How many dogs and cats had had those accessories removed surgically?

I tugged harder, determined to succeed at this Barbie thing, and Lacy's head popped right off.

"I'm so sorry." I held the two pieces close to me, afraid I would traumatize Katie if she saw them.

Katie didn't miss a beat. "See, she's cranky." She took the doll and wrestled the head in place.

It was a little disturbing to watch, but I kept my mouth shut.

Finally, once both of our dolls were properly dressed and groomed, it was time for them to go to the kitchen for tea and cookies. Katie insisted that the Barbies walked there, so I crouched down and tipped Lacy from side to side to imitate walking.

Katie did the same, all the while talking for Lacy and her doll, Cami.

"You look so pretty. Can I borrow your dress?"

"Sure. But I want to try on your shoes."

I cleared my throat. "Where did you get that purse?" I asked in a high-pitched voice.

Katie stopped moving and stared at me. I felt like the guy in the movie theater who forgot to turn his phone off and gets a text twenty-five minutes in.

Realizing that I was not doing the voice right, I kept quiet as I followed her into the kitchen.

We sat our dolls on the countertop and began to scour the room for teacups and saucers. We filled up Evie's teakettle with water, and Katie found a container of cookies in the pantry.

We set the cups up on the island and plated cookies for everyone. Just as we started our tea party, I heard a soft laugh coming from the doorway.

I startled and turned to see Penny standing there with her arms crossed and her eyebrows raised. Instantly, I shot her an apologetic look. She'd told me no sugar, but I couldn't help it. Katie had been so excited about finding the cookies.

"Having fun?" she asked, her voice soft and—I wanted to believe—flirty.

I shrugged. "I never knew what I was missing until I discovered Barbies."

Penny looked amazing in my t-shirt and shorts. Her hair was damp and fell behind her shoulders. She looked refreshed, her cheeks pink. The t-shirt was too big, and the shorts came well past her knees, but all I could think about was wrapping her up in my arms and holding her close.

Feeling her soft curves against my body.

My entire face heated as I cleared my throat and turned my attention to Katie. She hadn't noticed her mother or my embarrassed expression. Instead, she was feeding cookies to Cami and talking in her adorable little voice.

"Can I join?" Penny asked. Her voice was closer, and when I turned, I found her standing next to me. She had her hands up and was combing her fingers through Katie's hair.

Katie was more than thrilled to set another place for Penny. She instructed me as we gathered another saucer and cup.

I wasn't sure how long we played Barbie tea party, but when Katie's eyes began to grow heavy, Penny moved to scoop her up into her arms and smiled over at me.

"It's time to put this princess down," she said.

I nodded as I stood as well. "You can lay her down in my room," I said before I thought it through.

Penny's eyes widened and then she shook her head. "No, that's okay. We'll take the guest room next to Evie. I don't want Katie to get lost if she looks for me."

I nodded as heat permeated my body. "Right. Of course." I had more fun at this tea party than I'd had at any Hollywood event. There was a peace, contentment even, that had evaded me for the last few years. It was why I'd come home looking for closure.

I studied Penny. The way she held Katie close and kissed her hair was so tender—it was everything I'd ever wanted in life.

It was right there in front of me and so far out of reach.

I shoved my hands into my front pockets and glanced around. What was I supposed to do here? If I was Katie's dad, I'd help Penny put her to bed.

But I wasn't. And I wasn't sure how Penny would react if I attempted to take on that role, even for one night.

Penny spoke softly, "I'd love some hot cocoa."

There was a look in her eyes. One that I hadn't seen before. One that got my heart pumping and made me feel like I could break down any wall to protect her.

One that told me she wanted to see me. Talk to me. Be around me.

I nodded and watched as she slipped out of the room.

The urge to please her took over, and I pulled every cupboard open in search of hot cocoa. Thankfully, Gran had some tucked in the very back. I refilled the kettle and set it to boil. After finding some mugs, I dumped the powdered mix into them and waited for the kettle to ding.

Marshmallows! Penny loved them. I did another search and found some in the pantry. I dropped a handful into each mug and then blew out my breath. There had been something in Penny's gaze. Something that had my nerves on edge. My stomach twisted in knots, and I wasn't sure what I was going to do.

Except worry.

Penny came in a few minutes later with her hair pulled up—exposing her long, sexy neck—and a soft smile on her lips. It had been a while since I'd seen a look like that from her. She'd been nothing but distant to me since I'd walked back into her life. But tonight, something was different.

"Smells amazing," she said as she padded over to me and lifted a mug. With both hands wrapped around it, she took in a deep breath.

"Well, I did work hard to make it," I teased. I needed to test the waters. Was she really opening up to me? Or was it all my imagination?

Penny glanced up as she sipped on the hot chocolate. Then she smiled and nodded toward the front door. "Should we go sit outside?"

I swallowed and slowly nodded. Sitting outside when we were kids meant something very different than what I was sure she meant now. Being outside meant being alone. Being alone meant…

My skin flushed as I pushed those thoughts from my mind. Thinking like that was not what I should be doing. "Sure," I said with as much confidence as I could muster.

Penny turned and headed toward the door. I followed after her as I tried to gather my thoughts. We were trying to be friends. The last thing I needed was to go and mess this all up.

The cool evening air surrounded us as we stepped out onto the porch. Penny left the front door cracked—just in case anyone woke up—and then we both wandered over to the rocking chairs and sat.

Penny brought her feet up onto the seat and rested her mug on one knee. She rested her head behind her as her gaze drifted around the yard.

I couldn't help but stare at her. It was a marvel that she was so calm when I was all over the place. What had changed? Had I missed it?

I was so confused and worried, that my entire body was a mess. Not able to sit still anymore, I stood and began to pace.

I wanted to be here—oh, how I wanted to be right next to Penny—but I still didn't know if she was with Tag. I didn't know if she even wanted me. She was hot and cold all the time, and I feared I'd mess up the one thing I'd worked so hard to restore—Penny's faith in me.

"Are you okay?" she finally asked.

I stopped moving and peered down at her. No. I wasn't okay. But how did I say that without upsetting her?

Her brows furrowed as she studied me. Then she set the mug down and stood. That movement brought her inches away from me, and she startled but didn't move. Instead, she just peeked up at me from under her ridiculously long eyelashes.

"Are you worried about your grandma?" she asked. Her voice was soft and caring, and I wanted to believe it wasn't the voice she used as a nurse. I wanted to believe that seeing me upset had brought out something more than simply her caring instincts or desire to heal those who were hurting.

I shook my head but then paused and nodded. "Well, yes and no. Yes, because I always worry about her. And no, because I know she has the best nurse in all of South Carolina."

She raised her eyebrows. "Just South Carolina?"

I winked and shrugged. "Okay, let's say the world?"

Penny chuckled as she studied me. Then her expression grew serious, and a moment later, she moved to walk away.

Without thinking, I grabbed her hand. I wanted her to stay. I was tired of us walking away from each other. I had so much I wanted to say to her, but I couldn't when she was constantly leaving.

"Penny..." I whispered, startled by the depth of my voice.

Penny kept her gaze downturned, but she didn't leave, which I took as a good sign.

"Are you with Tag?"

My question hung in the air. Penny's shoulders tightened as I saw her close her eyes for a moment and then tip her head to the side to study me. Finally, she let out her breath and faced me.

"No," she whispered.

Relief and frustration coursed through me. The opposing forces made my insides feel like I was walking on the deck of a ship in the middle of the ocean. I furrowed my brow as I held her gaze.

"Why did you lie to me?"

Penny's eyes filled with tears. She was hurting, and even though I was frustrated, the only thing I wanted to do was to take her pain away.

"I...had to," she said through a sob. A tear ran down her cheek, and I lifted my fingertips to wipe it away.

"Why did you have to lie?" It killed me inside that she felt like she needed to save face in front of me. Like I was going to judge her or something.

My own life was a wreck. I had to have my agent arrange a relationship for me. I was hopelessly in love with Penny, and because of that, I couldn't see past her to anyone else.

Penny was my destiny.

"Chris...I..." Her eyes widened with each stuttered attempt.

I held her gaze, weighing inside of myself how much I needed an answer to my question. I was sure she had her reasons, and I hated seeing that struggle inside of her. If I forced her to tell me now, would she regret it in the future?

Her lips trembled as she dropped her gaze to my chest. This was not what I wanted. Not after our amazing time at the beach, then with Gran, and then, lastly, with Katie.

I had to believe that Penny would tell me—that I would earn her trust—eventually.

So, I stilled the emotions inside of my chest and did the only thing I'd wanted to do since I got here. Since I'd seen her across the ballroom at the charity fundraiser. I pressed my fingers under her chin to tip her face up toward mine.

I held her gaze for a moment before I gently brushed my lips against hers.

She didn't respond, and fear gripped my chest as I pulled back to meet her gaze. Another tear rolled down her cheek as she stared at me. And then, suddenly, she rose up onto her toes, smashing her lips against mine.

Taking that as permission, I wrapped my arm around her waist and pulled her into me. My other hand found the base of her neck, and I threaded my fingers into her hair. Every part of me wanted to feel every part of her.

Penny responded by trailing her hands up my arms to my shoulders and then to my neck. She pulled me closer to her as if she feared I might disappear.

That was one thing she would never have to worry about. I wasn't going anywhere. Ever again.

I pushed her back gently until I felt the siding of the house against my palm. I pressed into her, using the support of the exterior wall. Our lips parted, and we fell into a dance. One that was familiar and yet brand new,

I remembered kissing Penny in the past. But this Penny... This Penny was someone completely different. She was a woman, and I was a man.

And there was this deep, primal part of me that wanted to show her I'd changed. I'd grown up. I would face my responsibilities. I'd be the man she'd dreamed about.

Just as I was about to fall in love with Penny all over again, she pulled back. I straightened so I could glance down at her. Our mingled breath was deep as we stood there not talking.

"Penny?" I asked, worried I'd done something wrong.

Her palms rested on my chest, and a moment later, she pushed me back. I obeyed only to watch her duck her head and hurry toward the door.

"Penny?" I called out, confused. Worried. Hurt that she was walking away. Again.

"I'm sorry, Chris," she said over her shoulder. "I'm sorry. I shouldn't have..." Her voice trailed off as she brought her gaze up to meet mine for a moment before a sob escaped, and she covered her mouth. "We can't."

With those two words lingering in the air, she pulled open the front door and disappeared inside.

I wasn't sure how long I stared at the door after she left, but it felt like an eternity. I didn't want to admit it, but a part of me hoped that she would come back out. That she would say she didn't mean what she'd said.

That she would allow me to hold her and kiss her like she deserved.

That she would let me love her like I so desperately wanted to.

But she never came back. Instead, I was the idiot who stood out on the porch all night, waiting.

13

PENNY

I locked myself in the guest room with Evie's monitor and bawled like I hadn't done in years.

The tears were as cleansing as they were exhausting. I cried for the girl I used to be, for the loss of her innocence and her childhood and the choices she'd had to make. I cried for the pain forced upon her when Chris left and for the hope I'd always held onto that he still loved me.

I finally fell asleep with one thought on my mind.

I think he loves me.

I woke to the same words floating around in my mind. They wouldn't leave me alone. Instead, they stayed at the forefront in large neon lettering. Add that to the way he'd kissed me with wild abandon, and I was a confused mess of a woman.

How was I ever going to move forward? How could I forget the way he'd held me like he never wanted to let me go?

Like he needed me more than air.

I was too overwhelmed to think clearly. Too caught up in the merging of past and present, lost love and new hope, to be anything more than an emotional wreck.

I managed to avoid Chris as I got ready. Katie was still fast asleep on the bed, and I got a text from Carter saying he was planning on stopping by. Evie woke up as Carter and I talked about the medicine I'd given her and how long she'd slept.

She lifted her hand, and I grabbed it, grateful to see some life in her. Grateful for the distraction caring for her gave me. "Morning," I said with a smile.

She barely smiled back at me. "I feel like I've been dragged behind a horse," she said, her voice raspy.

I grabbed the cup I'd placed beside her bed and helped her drink from the straw.

"What's the verdict, doc?" she asked Carter.

He patted her knee. "I think you're going to make it. We're going to stay on top of the meds and make sure you get plenty of rest."

She nodded once and closed her eyes. "Sounds good."

I followed him out the door and closed it behind us. "Tell me the truth," I demanded.

Carter checked his watch. "It's a virus, and it needs to run its course. But she's strong—all things considered—and I don't anticipate any problems. If her temp goes up, call me immediately. If it goes down, text."

I hugged him and was grateful when he returned the gesture and patted my back. Tears sprang to my eyes, and I looked up, willing them not to fall. I couldn't help the sniffle though.

"You okay?" he asked, touching my arm.

"I'm just tired. It was a long night." I swiped under my eyes, grateful I'd washed off my makeup last night. Then again, it would be nice to have something to cover up my tearstained face and bloodshot eyes. I probably looked like the monster that crawled out from under the bed.

"You need to get some rest. What time does the other nurse come?"

I lifted his wrist and checked his watch. "In about an hour."

"You need rest, doctor's orders." He patted my shoulder and then headed for the door.

What I needed was grounding. I needed to pull out Nurse

McKnight and Mommy and fall back into those rolls—where I was safe.

Where I was sure of my path even if I wasn't truly happy.

I was lonely.

I was careful.

I wasn't me.

Evie's fever broke five minutes before my shift ended. I breathed out a prayer of gratitude and felt so much better about turning her over to Quinn again. She was a good nurse—if not an overly friendly one. But I knew I could trust her to follow Carter's instructions and take care of Evie.

I scooped up my sleeping princess and headed out, managing to avoid Chris completely.

Or maybe he was avoiding me.

It wasn't like I'd been kind. I'd kissed and run. At some point, we'd have to talk about that—or else he'd leave town and my wounds would stay open for the rest of my life.

I wasn't sure which one would hurt more.

The drive home was quiet. Katie looked out the window, her arms wrapped around her backpack and her cheek resting on the top of it.

I kept going back to the tea party we had with Katie. To the way Chris talked with her, teased her, and the smile she gave him. It was one I hadn't seen before, one she only had for him.

It looked a lot like his. The swoop of their bottom lips was the same. The way they automatically showed all their teeth. I don't know how he didn't see a mirror when he looked into her face. The moment was so perfect, I felt completely unworthy to be a part of it.

I pushed all that away and decided to spend my day off re-centering myself. That started with making muffins with my princess.

We were just pulling them out of the oven when Lottie stumbled in, her pajamas crinkled and her eyes full of sleep. "I'm starving."

Katie giggled. "Your haiwr is cwazy, Auntie."

Lottie patted her head. She must have just pulled out her bobby pins and crashed last night. She grinned at Katie and flopped her stiff hair around to make her laugh.

"When did you get into town?" I asked as I set a plate with a single muffin in front of her and Katie. Jaxson, Lottie's boyfriend—and soon to be fiancé, if I was reading things right—was best friends with our brother Liam. They played pro football for the Wolves—a team based in Texas. Practices started a couple weeks ago, and Lottie and Jaxson were learning to navigate the waters of a long-distance relationship. I had no doubt they'd make it work and make it look easy.

Lottie yawned as she pulled the liner off the muffin. "Late. I'm not even sure what time."

She took a bite and moaned. "I missed homemade food though. Jaxson's trainer put him on an eating plan"—she shoved in another bite—"and I was trying to be supportive, but I've decided I need carbs to be happy."

I set another muffin on her plate and scooted the butter closer.

"Bless you," she said through her bite, spraying crumbs across the counter.

Katie tried to imitate her aunt, and I pointed a warning finger at Lottie. "Princesses don't talk with their mouths full."

With that statement, I dropped into the role of responsible mother. Only it wasn't as comfortable as I wanted it to be. It didn't fit the same. Because the old me would have shoved a muffin in my mouth and shot crumbs at Lottie.

And we would have laughed together—like sisters being silly.

I moaned and laid my head on the counter, my arms stretched out across the cool stone.

"Katie," Lottie said, "do you want to play beauty parlor in my bathroom?"

I lifted my head to see Katie's round eyes. "Yes." She nodded so deeply her chin hit her chest.

"Go on up. I'll be there in a few minutes."

I didn't even have it in me to point out the mess my little girl could make with Lottie's makeup.

"Relax, mama—that's what bathtubs are for." Lottie knew me too well.

I stood up and reached for the uneaten half of Katie's muffin. "Or high-pressure hoses, depending on what you have in that drawer."

She lifted a shoulder. "All the good stuff is in my suitcase still. She'll never find it."

I took some solace in that. I started putting away ingredients, and Lottie came around to unload the dishwasher. "Are you okay? You seem...down." She stacked the plates and put them in the cupboard.

My little sis was perceptive. If there was ever a word to describe my mood, it was *down*. "I kissed Chris last night."

A plastic container hit the floor, and Lottie grabbed my shoulders. "You kissed Chris Hartman?" She let out a squeal. "Is he as good of a kisser as I think he is?"

I swatted her hands away. "What are you talking about? You're with Jaxson."

"I know." She pulled her hands to her chest, "But Chris is so hot in his hero movies. I've always had a small crush on him."

"Lottie, stop!" I waved my hands. "You cannot crush on Chris." The more I thought about that the worse it sounded. "It would be like me crushing on Jaxson."

She snorted. "It's so not the same thing. For one, Jaxson is practically part of the family. You've always looked at him as a brother."

At the mention of family, the pressure of my secret grew. Like watching the red line on a thermometer go up and up—the longer she spoke, the less control I felt.

"...lived in this house," she continued.

"He's Katie's father," I blurted out and then clapped my hand over my mouth.

Lottie's mouth hung open. She stared at me, unblinking.

Oh the relief! I smiled. I couldn't help it. Having the truth out there where my sister could look it over and understand it was like taking the lid off a boiling pot. There was this burst of steam and then calm.

But right after the calm, the water started churning again. Right along with my stomach.

"Don't tell anyone," I begged. Now that I'd said the words out loud,

I almost wished I could take them back. Almost, but not quite. I'd carried that information, hiding it from my family, for so long it was like scar tissue, hard and unyielding, painful.

Lottie closed her mouth and pressed her lips into a thin line. Processing this big of a declaration took a minute.

I could only imagine what my parents would do.

"Okay. So. Okay." She picked up the dropped container. "Wow."

"Yeah. Wow." I grabbed the silverware basket, needing to keep my hands busy as I talked. And talk I did. I started at the very beginning, the first day Chris and I snuck out of school and shared mint chocolate chip ice cream on the bridge over Moss Lake. I told her how I fell in love with him, and how his mom died and he left town. How I knew he needed to go because everything here reminded him of her and how I didn't know—was too young to know—how to help him mourn.

She listened intently, seeing the past with new eyes. She was five years younger than me and had missed out on a lot of conversations between me and Mom.

"But why didn't you tell him when you found out you were pregnant?" She rested her chin on her fist and set her elbow on the counter—the dishwasher long forgotten.

I traced my finger over the marble countertop, following a vein of color. "I was going to. I called to tell him, but when he answered the phone, he said he was just about to call me—he'd gotten the part. He was so happy. I hadn't heard that much joy in his voice in months. What was I supposed to do? Tell him to leave it all behind and come home?"

Lottie patted my hands. "Yeah, but…"

"For a while I told myself I'd tell him the next time he called. And then his calls got farther apart, and life got complicated and I had to let him go." I swallowed the lump in my throat.

Lottie closed her hands around mine. "You have to tell him."

"No." I leaned back, breaking contact. "No. Uh—no." I couldn't seem to say the word enough, and it was stuck on repeat.

Lottie grabbed my face in her hands. "He's her dad—he deserves to know."

I shook my head. "What if he takes her away?" The words came out strained because my throat was closing off.

She pulled her hands away and deflated into her chair. "That is not cool."

"See." I sat next to her.

"But you kissed him."

I groaned. "Momentary lapse in judgement."

"Was it?"

"No—I wanted to." Oh my gosh, I'd wanted to kiss him with every molecule in my body. When he'd looked at me that way, like I was his world and the universe wrapped in diamonds and rubies, I'd lost all sense of self-preservation.

She twisted in her seat so our knees bumped. "You've been living with scary what-ifs since Katie was born. Have you given any thought to the positive ones?"

"Like?" If she started talking about the benefits of child support I was out.

"Like, what if you guys worked it out? He's not just starting out anymore."

I shook my head. "His career comes first. Everything he's done since he left here has been for his career."

She gave me a look. "Actors have families, Pen." She paused and then went on. "You're both established now. He's paid his dues, and you have a career. It might work."

Hope, small and untested, vulnerable and tender, sprouted in my heart. "Maybe," I answered, unable to give her a full commitment. "I'll think about it." Like I could think about anything else.

Katie swooped into the kitchen. "I'm beautiful!" She threw her hands above her head and batted her eyelashes. Her eyelids were smeared in purple and hot pink, she had orange cheeks, and red lipstick on her teeth and around her mouth. The front of her shirt was covered in a rainbow of fingerprints and swipes.

Heaven help me.

Probably sensing that I was already overwhelmed, Lottie jumped up. "All mermaids, get ready for a swim party."

Katie clapped her hands. "Can I bring my Barbies?"

"It's not a party if you don't. Let's get our suits on." Lottie ushered her back up the stairs. She turned at the bottom and blew me a kiss. "Positive what-ifs."

I rolled my eyes. "I'll try."

I laid down on the counter, feeling tired and worn through but relieved. Relieved that I was no longer the only keeper of the truth. Telling my secret had set me free. Well, with Lottie. There were so many others who deserved to know.

Starting with Chris and ending with Mom and Dad.

Maybe not Dad…He was hugely protective of his girls.

Even the black sheep.

I moaned and got up to finish emptying the dishwasher.

One image kept coming to mind. It was when Chris put his hand on Katie's back, and she smiled up at him. I couldn't deny the connection there—that they were meant to be together.

And maybe, just maybe, we were meant to be a family.

14

CHRIS

I carried a tray into Gran's room, watching carefully to make sure the chicken noodle soup didn't spill over the edge of the bowl and onto the crackers.

Gran was sitting up in her hospital-style bed. When she wanted to come home from the hospital, I asked them what she needed to be comfortable and safe. An adjustable bed was on the top of the list. I handed over my credit card number and told them to set her up.

Seeing her now, tired but comfortable with her hands folded in her lap, made it worth every penny.

"Here we go." I set the tray over her lap and stopped to kiss the top of her head. Her hair smelled like dry shampoo. Quinn refused to let Gran out of bed for a bath, no matter how much she insisted she needed to feel clean to get better.

"I'll bet you're ready for Penny to come back," I said with a chuckle.

"Not as much as you are." Gran lifted the spoon and took a dainty sip of the broth.

"What makes you say that?"

She pointed to the monitor on her bedside. "These go both ways. Didn't you know?"

I froze as I was instantly reminded of how much Penny and I had said last night. Were kissing sounds loud enough to be picked up by the speaker? Then I felt stupid. Of course they were. That's what we had boom mics for on set.

My face heated.

She continued to eat slowly, savoring each bite. Or maybe she was forcing it down. Either way, it did my heart some good to see her eat.

"Let me ask you something." Gran dabbed at the corners of her mouth with a napkin. "What's your goal here?"

"To make sure you're healthy and strong."

Gran waved that away. "That's your excuse. What did you really come home for?"

I considered making another joke. Speaking like this, open and unabashed, wasn't going to help me with my goal of burying my feelings for Penny. I'd worn my emotions on my sleeve only to have her run—literally—away from me.

But Gran wasn't having any of it. She already knew the answer to her question—asking me was just a formality. Plus, I loved my grandmother and didn't want to beat around the bush with her.

I ducked my head and sighed. "Closure, I guess. I'm supposed to marry Jackie, but...I feel lost."

Gran's eyes sparkled. "How's the closure going?"

A laugh burst out of me. It felt good to release some of the pressure that had built up inside. "Not as good as I'd hoped."

She folded the napkin and then folded it again. "Let me give you some advice. Before you go chasing after that girl, consider the next phase and the one after that."

I pulled my eyebrows together, wondering where she was going with this.

"Being a mom changes women. We can't follow some cute actor back to Hollywood on a whim."

"Penny's not a whim." She never had been. She was the one constant in my life. The woman who outclassed, out-loved, and outshined every starlet and model I'd had on my arm.

Gran pressed her palms together and looked up thoughtfully. After a pause, she reached over and covered my hands. "Your love is commendable. But you have to think of her."

"That's the one thing I'm not struggling with doing." I grinned.

Gran grinned back, but the light in her eyes was dimmer, full of concern instead of the joy I thought she'd feel. "Don't play with her heart. She has a life here, and her family is close. I don't think you can pull her away from them."

The statement had me reining in my reckless thoughts. I knew there was truth to what Gran had said, but there was a part of me that wanted to cling to the hope that everyone—including myself—could be wrong. "It wasn't that way before," I said in a lame attempt to protect myself.

"She's been through a lot since you left."

Change seemed to be the theme of my life lately. Facing it. Accepting it. And now I contemplated making it. Sweeping Penny and Katie into my life in California was exactly what I'd planned on doing. I had major parts coming my way; the kind that would put me on the same level as Harrison Ford and Sean Connery.

But Gran's words cut against that plan. I'd always figured Penny would come with me. But now, the idea of asking her to leave her life felt...selfish.

I frowned. There was more to consider here than my heart.

I scrubbed my face. Even though I knew what Gran was saying was right, I couldn't just jump on board. There had to be a way for Penny and me to be together. We had to at least try. Right? And if protecting Penny from getting hurt was Gran's biggest worry, I could put that to rest in a heartbeat.

"I'll be careful," I promised Gran.

She studied me and then sighed. I could tell she was already tired out.

I stood up and took the tray off her lap. "I'll take care of this; you get some rest."

"I'm fine." She lifted a few fingers off the blanket, her eyes already drifting shut.

I made my way out to the kitchen, where I rinsed the dishes and loaded the dishwasher.

Just as I started the dishwasher, Quinn came in with a huge smile on her face. "There's someone here to see you." She practically sang the words.

Expecting Penny, I hurried around the island. "Show her in." I couldn't believe I had to tell Quinn that. Why was Penny being shy?

The click-clack of high heels told me something was different. Maybe she'd come to ask me out to lunch? I looked down, brushing the front of my shirt in case I had crumbs from doing dishes. I looked up just as a pair of willowy arms wrapped around my neck and the scent of expensive perfume hit my nose.

"Jackie?" I hugged her out of reflex.

She giggled and nuzzled her face into my neck. "I've missed you, dreamboat."

I cringed at her nickname as I pushed her away from me, keeping my hands on her sides to keep her from getting any closer. "What are you doing here?"

"I'm not alone." She turned and motioned to Bailer who was grinning like the lion who caught the gazelle.

"Bailer, how's it going?" I moved Jackie to the side and went over to shake hands.

"I've never been better. You are going to be so happy I came today." He motioned to the table, and we all took seats. Jackie pulled hers closer to me. The sound of doors opening had me turning around to find Quinn staring at all of us. At least her phone wasn't in her hand.

"We'll be just a minute," I said.

"Okay." She looked unimpressed as she made her way down the hall, hopefully to check in on Gran.

"What's going on?" I glanced back and forth between the two of them. They sat on either side of me with too-happy expressions. I suddenly felt like I'd walked right into a trap.

Bailer pulled a stack of papers from his ever-present briefcase. "I have an offer for you—for the Guy Wonder part."

"No way!" I offered him a fist bump. I'd read the script two years ago and had been campaigning for the lead ever since. This would be the role that went down in cinematic history like Luke and Indiana.

"There's a catch." Bailer's eyes darted to Jackie and away.

My stomach sank. I could guess what the catch was—Indiana always needed a leading lady, and the studio and fans loved to see me and Jackie come together on and off the screen.

"They want a married couple to play the part."

I schooled my features. I was an actor, after all, and all the world was a stage—especially in front of Jackie. A revelation hit me—that's what was missing in my relationship with her, the real me. I'd been *on* every time we were together. No wonder I was exhausted by the thought of marrying her.

Thoughts of Penny floated through my mind. She was the one person I didn't have to act for. She knew me. The real me.

I wanted to stay. I wanted to be here to figure out where things were going with us, but I couldn't stop the nagging feeling that pulled at the back of my mind. The one that said me staying wasn't what Penny wanted.

Gran didn't believe in us. She'd all but said those words earlier. Could I put everything I'd worked toward on the line for a solid maybe?

Especially when my dream felt like a nightmare for Penny.

She hadn't been shy about her desire for me to leave since the moment I stepped foot back in Evergreen Hollow.

Plus, it wasn't like I could shut this down—I'd dreamed of this part for too long. But I had to play it cool. With Jackie sitting next to me, one wrong word, one strained tone, could blow the whole thing up in my face.

The problem was, I didn't know who had orchestrated this ambush. I'd suspect Jackie—she was the one who would benefit the most—but it could have been Bailer who'd invited her along. He knew I'd been out of sorts lately and was back in Evergreen Hollow to put some demons to rest. He might have sent her here as a shield—a way to protect himself from me backing out of the deal we'd worked on for two years.

I was in a pit of stinking vipers.

"If you'll excuse me for a moment?" I pushed my chair back and got to my feet. "I need some fresh air."

"Chris?" Jackie asked in a concerned and calm tone. "They only want us if we come together. My career is riding on this role too. We don't have a choice, really. We can't let our fans down."

Oh, she was good. Inside, she had to be freaking out. She wanted this as much as I did. The difference between us was that I wouldn't have tried to guilt trip her into it. I wouldn't hitch my wagon to her star and then try to steer.

I walked out the front door without saying another word. I brushed off my arms as if I'd stepped through a spider web and the threads had stuck to my skin.

I breathed in deeply. Gran's warning and this opportunity built a crazy quilt that I had to somehow piece together and make into my life.

Tires crunched on the drive, and I looked up to see Penny's car pulling in.

I stood in front of the door, feeling like a shield between what was inside and what was on the way in.

There was no way I could keep my two worlds from crashing together.

I just hoped the explosion didn't destroy everything sweet between me and Penny. But how could I be the actor Chris Hartman *and* the man she needed me to be?

15

PENNY

Needing a buffer between me and Chris, I'd impulsively told Katie she could come to work with me today. Once that girl got an idea in her head, it was hard to get it out. She packed herself a bag of Barbies and camped by the door.

I finished my makeup and rethought things. Katie could be in the way, and Gran was still recovering. One look at my girl with her hands clutching the straps of her backpack, her eyes alight, told me that I didn't have the luxury of backing out. If I changed my mind now, the result would be fits and screams. I couldn't leave my mom with a four-year-old's emotional mess to clean up, especially since she'd complained of a headache and gone to her room right after breakfast.

Thankfully, Katie seemed content to fill the silence in the car with her chatter. She was going on and on about the show she watched this morning while I prepared myself to see Chris again.

I pulled into the driveway and found Chris standing near the fountain with a very confused look on his face. Whatever he was going through, I didn't want to be a part of it. And spending my time taking care of Evie and running after Katie ensured that there would be no opening for him to tell me. Score one for bringing the kid.

I could feel his gaze on me as I stuffed the car keys into my purse, looped the strap over my shoulder, and climbed out of the car. I hurried to the back door to let Katie out, but she beat me to it. As soon as her feet hit the ground, she sprinted over to Chris.

My complaint about her not waiting for me never left my lips as I watched Chris crouch down and scoop her up into his arms. He pulled her up so they were eye level, and he studied her as she told him all the important things that happened this morning.

Whatever was ailing him when I first pulled in must have subsided because he was all smiles for that little girl. He held her close as she tipped her lips to his ear and began to whisper.

Even though I was still a jumble of nerves after our kiss, the scene playing out in front of me was too adorable not to smile at. I attempted to hide it as I retrieved her backpack from the back seat and shut the door. I slung the bag over my shoulder and turned, taking in a deep breath as I readied myself for a conversation with Chris.

What was I going to say? How does one have a normal conversation with their ex-boyfriend with whom they just shared a mind-blowing kiss? Adding to my confusion, that person just happened to be the father of my child and didn't know it.

Wow, when I laid it out in my head like that, I began to realize just how messy my life had become. I was like my grandmother's yarn after her cat Bumbles got to it. I didn't know where the tangle began, and from where I was standing, the end didn't exist.

I was so wrapped up in my lies and trying to keep the truth from Chris—from myself—that I had lost sight of what I was doing and why.

"Is that so?" Chris asked as he tipped Katie away from his head so he could look her in the eye.

Katie's nod was solemn as she moved to continue whispering.

I was mesmerized, watching the two of them together. If I had been just a bystander, I would have assumed they'd known each other forever. I would have assumed they were father and daughter.

That thought created an ache so strong inside of me that it took my breath away. Would it be so bad for Chris to know? He clearly cared about her, and I had the feeling that if he knew, his love for her would only grow stronger.

Telling Lottie about Chris had felt like removing a brick from this backpack of lies that I'd been carrying around for far too long. Imagine if I told Chris about Katie? The weight would lessen substantially.

"Oh, here's where you ran off to," a loud, very familiar voice said from behind me.

I turned just in time to see Jackie cross the driveway and walk right up to Chris. I blinked a few times. When did she get here?

My blood began to boil as I rested my hands on my hips. I wanted to tell Chris off for inviting his on-again, off-again Hollywood fling into this situation. I wanted to scream at him. But I couldn't. Chris was no longer mine. If he wanted to bring in Jackie to help him remember that, yes, he had a life back in Hollywood that didn't include Katie and me, who was I to stop him?

Deflection wasn't a nice color on him, but it was an action I could relate to. After all, I'd pulled Tag into my mess when I couldn't face the truth. What was so different about this?

Chris and Katie stopped their conversation and turned to face her.

"My name is Princess Buttercup," Katie said in a shy voice. She extended out her hand while burying her face into Chris's neck. It was one of her defense mechanisms when she was nervous—telling people a fake name until she got to know them better.

Last night, I may have put on *The Princess Bride* while I drowned myself in peanut butter cup ice cream.

Jackie stared at Chris and then moved her gaze to Katie. She studied Katie's hand, noting the dried-on sticky syrup from breakfast glistening on her pudgy little fingers. She laughed uncomfortably.

"I don't touch…people," Jackie said with a flick of her black hair.

Momma bear rose up inside of me, and I all but growled as I took a step toward them. But before I could respond, Chris turned so his body was a shield between Jackie and Katie.

"You don't have to be rude. She's just a kid," he said in a low voice as he raised his hand up to shield Katie's ear.

Thankfully, one look at my daughter told me she'd lost interest. She patted Chris's back as if she were singing a song in her mind and needed to release the dance energy she felt.

During moments like these I was grateful that I'd raised such an imaginative kid. Nothing got her down for too long. Plus, it helped me know that Katie was doing exactly what she needed to do, be a kid and not get caught up in the drama unfolding around her.

"Come on, let's go inside and see Granny Evie," I said as I stepped forward and extended my hand.

I felt Jackie's startled gaze on me. Apparently, she hadn't even noticed I was standing a few feet away. Katie complained a few times —I even got a begging look from Chris as he lowered her to the grass —but I stood my ground and wrapped my hand around Katie's.

I didn't stop, even when I met Chris's gaze for a brief moment and saw the desperation inside of it. He wanted to talk to me, but I wasn't ready to hear it. I was pretty sure I wasn't ever going to be ready to hear it.

"Why did you run off? With news like that, I figured you'd be thrilled," I heard Jackie say as I guided Katie up the porch steps.

Out of instinct, I paused. News?

"Can we talk about this later?" Chris asked. His voice was low and chock-full of annoyance.

"Dinner?" Jackie's voice rose an octave.

I bent down and pretended to tie Katie's shoe. This allowed me to tip my face ever so slightly so I could see what they were doing. Jackie had flung herself into Chris's arms, her hands wrapped around his neck. She had her lips pouted and poised in his direction, should he decided to kiss her.

I felt like vomiting as I hurried with the shoelace. No longer able to stand there, listening and watching them, I grabbed Katie's hand and disappeared into the house. Once I was on the other side of the door, I shut it and collapsed against the hard oak.

I wanted to lock the door and never speak to Chris or *Jackie* ever again. My heart felt as if it had been broken into a million different pieces, and I was on the verge of tears. Big, fat, sucky tears.

I stifled a sob and felt Katie's hand surround mine. I felt like the worst mother ever. I couldn't keep my emotions in check. I couldn't be the mother Katie needed me to be. I couldn't believe the thought of being myself had entered my mind only a few days ago when I was on the beach with Chris.

Katie deserved all of me—even if that meant never finding love again. With my track record, I was going to make the same mistakes over and over again. If I was going to be happy—or, at least, Katie was going to be happy—I needed to give up on love.

Gathering all the strength that I had, I swallowed my emotions and opened my eyes. I glanced down at Katie and gave her the biggest, widest smile I could. She returned the smile only to have it morph into one of fear as she began to back away.

I softened my smile when I realized my overzealous effort may have freaked her out. I crouched down and pulled her into a hug. She nuzzled my neck and then pulled back to give me a kiss on the cheek.

"I love you, Mommy," she said, followed by another hug.

"I love you, munchkin."

"Chris?" A low, unfamiliar voice asked. A man in a pressed suit and dark curly hair rounded the corner and stopped dead in his tracks. His gaze focused on us, and an uncomfortable expression flashed over his face. "I'm so sorry, I thought you were Chris."

Katie pulled away and hid behind me as I straightened and held out my hand. Even though I was smiling, inside I was chanting my resolve to let all my thoughts of me and Chris go. I was going to be a gracious hostess to whoever this was.

"Penny McKnight, I'm here to take care of Mrs. Hartman."

The man studied me for a moment. "Ah, Chris's grandmother." He stepped forward and shook my hand. "I'm Bailer. I represent Chris."

He dropped his hand at the same time I did. I nodded and smiled. Katie whispered something from behind me, but I couldn't make it out.

We stood there in the silence, awkwardly glancing around. I wasn't sure what to say to Bailer, and it seemed that he felt the same.

Finally, Bailer cleared his throat and rubbed his hands together. "It's exciting, isn't it?"

Confused, I leaned in. "What?"

Bailer wiggled his eyebrows. "The movie. The relationship. It's good those two are getting back together. The tabloids will be thrilled, and the movie deals will keep rolling in."

The foyer felt as if it were closing in on me. I stared at him, trying to piece together what he'd said.

"I'm sorry, what?"

Bailer sidestepped me to peer out the side window. I could only assume he was studying the *perfect couple* out there.

"It's always refreshing when two incredibly talented, incredibly beautiful people get together, don't you think?" Bailer turned to me with a wide smile. My feelings about what he said must have shown because his smile faded as he studied me.

He returned his attention to whatever was happening outside. I sucked in my breath as I grabbed Katie's hand and headed toward the kitchen. I knew I should have been happy, after all, having Chris here had been hard, emotional, and confusing.

Hearing that I was going to get out of that should have made my day...but it didn't. My broken heart was hemorrhaging.

I needed to make sure I hadn't misunderstood. I turned to Bailer and swallowed as I readied myself for whatever answer he was going to give me.

"So Chris is moving back to Hollywood to marry Jackie?"

Bailer didn't turn his head right away to acknowledge my question, but when he did, his expression answered the question for me. But, like adding the last nail to the coffin, he parted his lips and said the one word that would shatter the small amount of happiness that I'd finally found.

"Yes."

16

CHRIS

I pulled Jackie off of me and stormed toward the house. The way she'd treated Katie and dismissed Penny had shown me her true colors. No woman in her right mind would look at Katie's adorable heart-shaped face and wrinkle her nose in disgust.

Therefore, Jackie was obviously not in her right mind.

"What's the matter?" She clomped after me, her arms flailing as if she couldn't keep her balance in a five-inch heel. She could—she did it really well on camera—just not while I was dodging her grasp. On screen, I was usually the one pawing at her.

My stomach curdled at the thought. I stopped suddenly, and she fell into me. Probably on purpose. I stumbled away and grabbed her wrists as she tried to wrap her arms around my neck again.

"What's with you? Can't I have five seconds without you trying to manhandle me?" I growled. Playing nice had been thrown out the window.

She stepped back, and I let go of her arms.

"Can you give me a chance to breathe?" I bent over and clutched my chest. I wanted to believe it was to catch my breath, but the pain inside of me had nothing to do with physical exertion and everything to do with the woman who had just gone inside.

Jackie's eyes glinted, hard and calculating. She cleared the look almost as fast as it had appeared, but I'd caught it. Caught it and catalogued it.

She tugged at her shirt hem. "I was only trying to show you I care." She'd made her voice smaller, her eyes doe-like.

"Yeah. Um…I need a minute or two alone to think things over."

"Isn't that what you've been doing?" She put a manicured hand on her hip. "You've been thinking for weeks. It's time to take action." She held up her hand in a fist.

I realized something. I wasn't the only one acting, she was playing a part too. "Jackie," I heaved out a sigh. "Can we just…be ourselves for a minute?"

"What do you mean?" She batted her eyelashes.

"That." I pointed at her. "That right there. Just stop acting like my girlfriend and be my friend." I felt so lost and confused. I wanted someone to be a sounding board for me to bounce things off of. If Jackie was going to be my wife, I would hope that that someone would be her. But right now, confessing my feelings about another woman to Jackie was the furthest thing from my mind.

Her eyebrows came together, and she bit her lip. But this time, I didn't see the same conscious effort in the expression. "I don't follow."

"Think about it for a minute." I pushed through the front door and almost tripped over Bailer. I stepped back as I swept my gaze around the room. Was Penny still here? Had she run into Bailer? What did he say to her?

My stomach sank faster than botched Botox.

Bailer seemed just as cool and collected as he had been when he first walked in. As if a ten-minute conversation was all it took to solve the issues between Jackie and me. "Are we all set?" He rubbed his palms together.

I considered him. Upbeat. Charming. Was it real or fake? How well did I really know this guy? How well did I know anyone?

My heart squeezed at that thought. The only person who knew me —really knew me—was somewhere in this house, not standing next to me in the foyer. Penny knew me, and I was pretty sure that I knew her.

She'd left me outside to deal with Jackie, but before she left, I was fairly confident that I could read her mind. Her piercing stare said it all. *You did this to yourself—you clean it up.*

"No. We're not. I'm not. Did you see where Penny went?"

Bailer blinked. "The nurse?"

"Yeah." I forgot she had dressed for work. She looked good in anything and everything.

"I think she went that way." He pointed down the hall.

I headed that direction, pausing to listen at Gran's closed door. Katie's excited chatter came through, and I grinned. That little munchkin had grabbed my heart with both of her syrup-covered hands as she'd whispered about Sweet Westley. Tristoff might get a run for his money with the Dread Pirate Roberts entering the little girl's heart.

I went inside and found Gran and Katie on the bed, watching an animated movie. They seemed so comfortable sitting there, content with life and the universe and their places in it. They both looked at me, and Katie's eyes lit up. "Wanna watch?" She pointed to the television.

"I was actually looking for your mom."

"Oh, she's folding lawdry."

Gran seemed to melt into her bed with love for Katie. She snuggled her closer. "I think she's in the guest bedroom."

I nodded and left, the image of the two of them imprinted in my mind. That was what I wanted in life—so why was it so hard to find? I tried to imagine this life with Jackie, but that was an image even the best CGI artist couldn't create. Starting a family seemed far from Jackie's mind.

I went to the guest bedroom opposite mine and found Penny folding towels and sheets. "You don't have to do that," I said, leaning against the doorframe. "We have a maid come a couple times a week."

She jumped at the sound of my voice and laid her hand over her chest. "Geez. Give me some warning next time."

I gave her a sultry look instead.

Her cheeks turned rosy, and she went back to folding. "I don't mind. Monotonous tasks help me think things through."

I glanced down the hall to make sure I wasn't being followed before I stepped in and picked up a towel.

Penny lifted her eyebrows in question.

"What?" I teased. "You think you're the only one who has things to think about?"

She threw a bath towel at my chest. "What's on your mind?"

"Life. Choices. Paths." I tucked the towel under my chin and folded the corners together.

"I hear you're headed back to Hollywood."

"I don't know."

"Your agent seems to know."

"He believes what he wants to believe. It's a thing with agents. They have all this positive mental energy and talk big game when it serves their purpose."

"Do their plans ever pan out?"

"It did this time." I set the towel on a pile of them and reached for another. I wished I could reach for her, but her whole frantic energy thing was a huge neon *stay-away* sign. "There's this part—it's big. It's mine for the taking."

Penny paused, and for a moment, I wanted to believe that the drop in her expression was a result of what I'd said. But, as quickly as it came, her face returned to a forced smile. She glanced up at me. "So why aren't you packing?" she asked.

I studied her. Was she serious? "Because, I've realized there are other parts I want to play—no. That's not right." I crumpled the towel into a ball and then shook it out again. "I'm tired of always playing parts. I want to be real."

She blinked a few times. I wanted to tell her outright how I felt. There was so much I wanted to say, and I was tired of keeping it inside. But I also knew I couldn't just say it out loud. I knew she was prone to fearing the worst, and having her run off yet again wasn't something my heart—or pride—could handle.

She cleared her throat. "I saw your last movie. I don't think people saw you as playing a part. You looked…real." Her smile was forced as she tipped her face up to me.

I growled as I stared down at her, filling my gaze with as much emotion as I could. She knew what I meant. Why was she pushing me away? I'd been there last night. I'd felt that kiss. She wasn't fooling anyone with her coy attitude.

"That's not what I meant," I said, stepping closer to her. Inches separated our bodies. It took all of my strength not to reach out and pull her to me.

"Chris," she whispered. I could hear caution in her voice. It told me she knew what I meant. That there was a chance she felt the same.

"I want to be real…with you," I said softly as I ducked down to catch her gaze. She was staring a bit too hard at my chest.

"I…can't," she said as she lifted her chin. Tears filled her eyes. She blinked rapidly and swallowed.

"Why not?" I needed to know why she was fighting this. We were perfect together. I wanted her. All of her. And I wanted Katie. We could be a perfect family if she just let me in. I'd love Katie like my own—I'd already fallen for the little girl. If she was pulling away because of Katie's dad, she had to know I'd fight for them both.

"I…" Her voice drifted off, and she turned away from me. I could tell she wanted to say something, but she wasn't allowing herself to.

"If it's about Katie, you have nothing to worry about. I'll love her like my own."

A sob escaped Penny's lips. She hurried to cover her mouth, tipping her face forward as if to hide herself. Something was wrong. Really, really wrong.

Feeling out of my depth, I touched her elbow. "What is it?"

Penny kept her eyes pinched closed as she shook her head. I could feel the tug inside of her as she wrestled with whatever she wanted to tell me.

"Is it about Katie?" Was the truth that hard?

"There's something I have to tell you." She drew in a gasping breath. "It's just so hard. I've kept it in for so long."

I cupped her other elbow and turned her to face me. "Penny, whatever it is you can tell me. There are no secrets between us." I wanted her to know that. The ache inside of me—the one that wanted to protect her—had grown so bad that it was hard to breathe.

She was my person. It was as if I was born to protect her.

She barked a laugh and then bit her lip. "If you only knew," she whispered.

I searched her eyes. Her beautiful blue eyes. So much like Katie's. "Tell me," I urged quietly.

Her hands shook as she brought them up to trace my face. "I—" She cut off and looked down at my shirt instead. "Please don't hate me after I tell you this. I mean, you could. And I wouldn't blame you. But I'm hoping that you'll…I don't know."

"Penny." I shook her gently. "Just tell me."

"Katie…is yours," she whispered.

I stared at her lips. I knew that words had left her mouth, but my brain must have short-circuited because what she said couldn't be the truth. I blinked a few times as my entire body went numb. "I'm sorry, what?"

That couldn't be the truth. It just couldn't. There was no way she had kept this from me.

She looked up and met me eye to eye. "Katie is your daughter." She sucked in a breath. "You're her dad."

I stumbled backward and landed on the bed, knocking off the folded towels. I didn't make a move to pick them up. I was in such shock all I could do was open and close my mouth.

Katie.

Adorable, perfect, sweet, loving Katie was mine?

"I have a daughter," I said carefully, enunciating every syllable so there would be no miscommunication.

Penny nodded.

I stared at the ground as every emotion rose up inside of me. Anger. Betrayal. Pain. All of it filled my chest and coursed through me like an unstoppable snake, curling around all the happiness that I'd felt before and smothering it to death.

"Why..." I blinked as I tried to process what I wanted to say. I cleared my throat, closed my eyes, and drew in a deep breath. "You lied to me?" My tone was sharp. I winced as I attempted to soften my words. I knew she had her reasons; they just felt...unfair.

"I didn't lie," she whispered.

I glanced at her. Her lips were pinched together and regret smeared her face.

Didn't lie? Didn't *LIE*? Did she understand what a lie was?

"Let's go over the facts. You didn't tell me you were pregnant. Fine, I understand. We were over, and as much as it hurts that you didn't think I would do the right thing, you kept it to yourself. I can see that. But what about now?" Feeling the urge to move, I stood and began pacing.

"You told me Tag was Katie's dad. Then you said he wasn't. This whole time we've been together, you knew, and you kept it from me." I paused as I glanced down at her.

Tears fell as she nodded. "You're right. I have no excuse. It was a horrible thing for me to do. I was trying to protect Katie, but..." She closed her eyes.

"You didn't think about what this would do to me," I said, pointing to my chest.

She glanced up at me, another tear slipping down her cheek. "You're right. You deserved to know. I should have told you."

I nodded. "You should have."

I wanted to hate Penny right now, I really did. But no matter what, I still loved her.

I just couldn't forgive her.

Not right now at least. "I need to get out of here," I said as I moved to the door. I needed some fresh air and to be somewhere where the walls didn't feel as if they were smashing me like in the *Alice in Wonderland* movie that Gran and Katie were watching.

Penny stepped forward. "What about—"

"—Katie?" I finished for her. "I'll have my lawyer be in touch." I wasn't about to lose my daughter. Not after I'd just found her. No matter what happened between Penny and me, Katie wasn't going to suffer for my choices. She was mine, and from this moment on, she would know that.

I made my way back into the front room where Jackie and Bailer were waiting on the couch, surfing their phones. "We're leaving in ten minutes," I announced. "I need to get out of here." I breathed out.

They exchanged a look.

"I'll pack fast."

"I'll have the plane readied." Bailer started typing on his phone.

For once, Jackie didn't say anything. She didn't even try to pout or exploit the moment. She just gave me a sad little smile.

I hurried back to my room. I could hear Penny crying through Gran's door. I hoped she was telling Gran the truth—although I wondered if Gran already knew. How many times had she outlined my face when I was little—just like Penny had? It was because I had a heart-shaped face with a widow's peak. Or, I'd had one. Time had given me an edgier look. I prayed Katie would keep her chubby cheeks.

I threw things from my dresser into my large suitcase. I'd have someone come back and get whatever didn't fit. I had a movie to make, a career to take to the next level, and a custody case to file. I had no intention of taking Katie away from her mom and her extended family. All of me wanted her to grow up right here. But I would see her—by court order if necessary.

I threw open my bottom drawer and was greeted with a flash of neon orange. The whole world seemed to stop and hold its breath with me.

I reached for the ugly MORP polo shirt. The fabric was soft against my fingertips. My heart opened up—remembering the way Penny and I were back then. That was such a pure love; there wasn't any baggage attached—no personal traumas.

Just love.

The kind of love you use for a foundation to build a family.

My heart closed in on itself like a fist, and I bent double under the pain of it. Landing on the floor, I held the shirt close with one hand while I fished my wallet out of my back pocket with the other. I flipped it open and saw the tattered edge of an old bus ticket sticking up. I pulled it out and looked at it. I was such a fool. My life would have been so perfect if I'd just gotten on that bus to come home. I could have won Penny over back then. There wasn't as much time, as much damage, between us as there was now.

I should have shown up and refused to leave.

I should have been the man she'd needed me to be.

But I'd been broken, and I'd thought she wouldn't want me.

I folded the shirt and placed the ticket on top. Then I finished packing and rolled my suitcase into the hall. I stopped at the guest bedroom and picked up the towels I'd knocked over. They smelled like her. The whole house did.

One more reason to get out.

I laid the orange shirt with the ticket on top on the bed, hoping she'd understand my regrets.

Gran's room was quiet. I knocked softly, but there wasn't an answer. I poked my head in and found Gran asleep. Walking quietly, I leaned over the bed and pressed a kiss to her forehead.

Her eyes fluttered open and her hand came to my cheek. "You're leaving."

It wasn't a question. I nodded.

"Don't be a stranger and remember you are loved."

I touched her hand, leaning into her palm. "You too."

She kissed my cheek and then I tucked her back in.

I didn't see any sign of Penny or Katie, which was just as well. I didn't know if I could tell either of them goodbye. I felt like I was breaking some huge rule by walking out on them—even though I planned on coming back to see Katie as soon as my schedule would allow.

"The car's out front." Bailer took my luggage.

I slipped into the role of the cool Hollywood star who had the world at his feet. "Let's go."

I let him out first and then paused with my hand on the knob. "Goodbye," I whispered over my shoulder. Then I shut the door and strode confidently to the car.

"This is so amazing," said Jackie. "Our lives are just beginning."

I put on my sunglasses so no one would see the pain in my eyes and stared out the window as my family slipped through my fingers.

Regret filled my chest, but I muscled it down. I was doing the right thing. Penny didn't want me around so badly that she was willing to lie to me about Katie. So I was making it easy for her.

I was leaving so she could move on.

I was being kind to her even if it broke me inside.

17

PENNY

Katie knew something was wrong. Ever since Chris had walked out, I'd been a mess of tears and snot. I tried to put on a brave face, but nothing made me feel better. And my sweet, kind-hearted daughter could feel it.

Her mom was struggling.

"It's okay, Mommy," she said as she crawled into my lap.

I was an exhausted pile of a person on my bathroom floor. I'd managed to keep my emotions at bay while around Evie, but by the time I got home, my strength waned, and I hadn't been able to regain control since.

Tears slipped down my cheeks as I wrapped my arms around the anchor in my life and held her close. "I love you," I whispered.

Katie nodded and then wiggled until she was facing me. She placed her hands on both my cheeks and rose up until she was staring at me. "Did the Wicked Witch scare you again?"

When Evie had woken from her afternoon nap, she and Katie watched *The Wizard of Oz*. Katie had been mesmerized by Glinda and the Wicked Witch.

I rested my hands over Katie's and nodded. Yes, the Wicked Witch had scared me. Except in my situation, I was the wicked witch.

I was a horrible, awful person for lying to Chris for as long as I did. I cared about him, but I let fear and my own desire to protect my heart take over. He deserved so much better than how I'd treated him.

"I'm sorry," I whispered as I stared into Katie's sky-blue eyes. She furrowed her brow as she studied me.

She was most likely confused. I'd always taught her to say she was sorry when she'd done something wrong. In her sweet mind, I hadn't made a mistake, so why did I have to say sorry?

If she only knew.

I helped her up, and once she was in the tub, I moved over to sit on the toilet—easier access to the toilet paper. After I wiped all the tears and snot from my face, I took in a deep breath.

"Where's my Kate-ster?" Lottie's voice called from my bedroom.

I sat straighter as I patted my face. There was no way I wanted my sister to see me like this. She would know something was wrong and ask me about it. I'd only just now dammed the flow of tears, I didn't need her breaking down my meager attempt at composure.

"I'm in here, Awntie," Katie called. She'd arranged all of her Barbies on the edge of the tub.

"You are?" Lottie called, and a moment later, the door opened. "Where's your mo—" When her gaze met mine, she studied me for a moment and then turned her attention back to Katie.

They talked and played for a few minutes before Lottie excused herself and hurried from the room. I let out my breath as soon as she was gone. I ran my hands through my hair and closed my eyes.

How was I going to handle all of this? For the time being, I'd managed to throw Lottie off the scent, but that would only last for so long. It was the first time in a long time that I regretted living in such close proximity to my family.

It was hard to pretend when they were with you twenty-four seven.

Once Katie was washed and dressed, I curled up with her in her bed and read her a story until her eyes grew heavy, and she fell asleep. I stayed there for a bit longer, watching her breathe. I never felt more grounded than I did when I was with her. She was the reason I continued living. She was what helped heal my broken heart.

She was my world.

That thought only made me feel worse. I loved her so much, and yet, I'd selfishly kept her from the one man who would always protect her.

Realizing that my thoughts were beginning to spiral again, I forced back my tears as I kissed her once more, whispered another apology, and slipped from her bed. I padded over to my vanity, where I saw a sticky note taped to my mirror.

Kitchen. Now.

I didn't have to guess to know who wrote that.

Lottie.

She knew.

Taking in a deep breath, I threw on my robe for extra warmth and pulled open my door. I stilled my nerves as I made my way down the stairs and into the kitchen.

I almost turned to run when I saw Mom sitting with Lottie at the island, a carton of ice cream open between them. They spoke in hushed tones, and I couldn't help but think it was about me.

So many times in my teenage years, I'd overheard Mom and Dad discussing what they were going to do with their *problem child*. And, call me crazy, but I didn't want to hear that conversation ever again.

I wanted to say that I'd changed, but my behavior these last few days proved otherwise.

"There you are," Lottie said.

My entire body tightened as I watched my window to slip away slowly closed. I forced a smile and turned just in time to see Mom approach and wrap me in a hug.

And just like that, all the walls I'd built up disappeared, and I sobbed into her shoulder as she held me. I was so broken and hurting that all I could do was grip onto my mom. A few moments later, I felt Lottie's arms surround me.

I wasn't sure how long we stood there, holding each other, but it had to be a while or else I'd just cried so much that the tears I did have, only lasted a short while. I sniffled as I pulled away, and Mom and Lottie dropped their arms.

I could feel their gaze on me as I hastily wiped my cheeks with the bottom of my robe.

"Here," Mom said as she walked over to the tissue box that sat right next to the ice cream and pulled one out.

I thankfully took it and blew my nose.

Once we were situated around the island with the ice cream dished into bowls and covered in chocolate fudge, I took in their inquisitive stares.

I sighed. I was already on this truth kick, I might as well finish strong.

So I started at the beginning and didn't quit until I got to the events of this morning. I told them everything about Chris, my feelings for him, and the kiss we'd shared. When I finished, Mom and Lottie stared at me as if I'd just given birth to a baby giraffe.

My throat was hoarse from talking, and my eyes burned with so many tears. I focused in on my ice cream while they digested what I'd said.

"So, Chris Hartwell is Katie's dad?" Mom whispered.

I nodded.

"And he knows?"

I nodded again.

"How was the kiss?" Lottie asked.

I startled and, in the process, inhaled some of the melted ice cream. It tickled my throat, and I spent the next few minutes coughing.

"Charlotte," Mom scolded her.

I glanced over to see my sister shrug.

"What does that have to do with anything?" Mom asked.

Lottie laughed. "A kiss tells you a lot of things. If it was akin to kissing a dead fish, then I'd say there's no point in her trying to go after him. The romance is dead, and you two can be friends raising a daughter."

My cheeks heated as the memory of being wrapped up in Chris's arms flooded my entire body.

"But if there was electricity. If you felt as if you were drowning and kissing him was the only thing that would save you..." She fell silent as she studied me.

My entire body ached as her words slammed into me. That was exactly how I felt when he kissed me. That was exactly how I felt right now *thinking* about kissing him.

She narrowed her eyes as she took in the high color on my cheeks. "Looks like you need to go after him. You need to fight for him."

I dropped my gaze. I began to flatten the crushed tissue as a feeling of helplessness washed over me. "But I lied to him."

"I know." Mom patted my knee. "And it was wrong. But that's the beauty of mistakes—especially with a person who loves you unconditionally—they find a way to forgive you."

I glanced up at Mom's words. There was a truth to what she said. An experience I could see in her gaze. She knew what she was talking about. I had done some stupid things as a kid, and yet, she and Dad always found it in them to continue loving me, to move forward, to give me space to grow.

"Do you think he'll forgive me?" I asked, my voice so small hope could hardly fit inside of it.

"He loves you, Pen. Everyone can see it," Lottie said as she scooped up a spoonful of ice cream.

"They can?" I asked.

Lottie and Mom nodded in unison.

"What do I do?" I'd never felt so lost or confused. "He told me to give him space."

Mom stood up and wandered over to a drawer and pulled it open. She grabbed out a pen and a piece of paper.

"What are you doing?" Lottie asked.

"I'm making a packing list."

"A what?" Lottie and I asked together.

Mom sighed. "You always hated that he never came back for you. Even though I didn't know he was Katie's dad, I knew you felt abandoned. But you weren't in a place to go after him back then. You're not going to make the same mistake."

HIS SECRET BABY

Fear crept up inside of me as I digested Mom's words. "You want me to go after him?"

Mom shook her head. "Not just you. You and Katie. She needs to know the truth."

"Katie and me?"

"Ooo, good idea. No one can say no to that little munchkin," Lottie said as she tapped her hand on the countertop.

I swallowed. "I should tell Katie?" And then a resolve rose up inside of me as my emotions answered that question for me. "I should tell Katie."

Mom and Lottie stared at me like that was obvious.

"Tell Katie and then go after him. You love him, right?" Mom asked.

I nodded. Being this truthful felt so refreshing. I did love him. With everything inside of me and more. I loved him. "Yes."

Mom laughed and returned to writing. "Then it's settled."

"But does he love me back?" A wave of fear washed over my happiness. Was he going to be able to forgive me? Was it possible?

Just then, my phone chimed. I pulled it from my robe pocket and glanced down. It was a text from Quinn.

Evelyn wanted me to send this to you. I don't know why, but she won't take her medication until I do.

I chuckled. I could hear the annoyance in her words. I waited a few seconds and suddenly, a photo came through.

I blinked.

"Who texted you?" Lottie asked as she licked the ice cream off her spoon.

I glanced up with my eyes wide. It was a picture of the orange MORP polo shirt that he'd tried to throw away with what looked like a bus ticket lying on top.

I clicked on it so I could zoom in on the ticket. The date of departure was the day after Chris had left, and the destination?

Evergreen Hollow.

I squealed as I handed the phone to Lottie, who took it and stared at the photo.

"What is it?" Mom asked.

I couldn't speak as I collapsed onto the barstool.

"I dunno. It's some ugly shirt and what looks like garbage."

"Chris still loves me," I whispered.

Lottie looked up at me. "You got that from this photo?"

I nodded as I stood and pulled my sister up into a hug. "He loves me!" I squealed again.

"Ouch. That was my ear," Lottie said as she tried to slip from my arms.

I just held onto her for a moment longer before I let her go. She pulled out her phone and found me a flight around noon. After a hug with Mom—who shoved the packing list into my hand—I hurried up to my room and quietly entered. I busied myself with packing things for Katie and me.

My heart swelled with anticipation as I finally crawled into bed at four in the morning. I lay there, staring up at the ceiling. I giggled as I closed my eyes and the photo from earlier flashed in my mind. I couldn't wait for the sun to rise and for the morning to come.

Tomorrow, I would tell him the truth once more.

Tomorrow, I would tell Chris that I loved him.

18

CHRIS

A nasty storm blew against the coastline. Waves taller than roller coasters smashed into the beach outside my back door, roaring loud enough to wake the dead. Lightning glinted off the palm trees as they whipped in the wind, and rain pelted the windows.

"No wonder you can't sleep." Bailer came in wearing his college sweats.

I glanced at him. "Yeah." Though it wasn't the storm that kept me awake. It was the look in Penny's eyes as she'd left the guest room. I kept replaying the moment when she told me Katie was my daughter. Anguish had twisted her features. If I'd only taken a moment to look at her—really see her—the conversation would have gone differently, and I wouldn't be in the middle of this storm.

"I don't know what's darker—that sky or your face." Bailer came to stand next to me at the bay window. He folded his hands in front of him and rolled his shoulders. "I'm afraid to ask what's wrong, but it's part of my job description to keep you happy."

I dipped my chin to let him know I'd heard him, but I didn't have an easy answer. All those were taken away the moment I found out I had a daughter. No, not then. The answers were easy then. Becoming a family would have been so simple.

The hard part came when I realized Penny wouldn't have me.

I believed she wanted me. As the old song says, "You feel it in the kiss," or something like that. Penny couldn't fake what was between us. That wasn't possible. I couldn't muster up that much authenticity even for a lead part. I wish I had those skills.

But I knew Penny didn't. She'd never been able to act. Her audition for the school play was so bad, they made her a tree—and that was only because her father was the main sponsor.

Bailer tried again. "This part will be a gamechanger. Enjoy these last few days of peace because your career is going to—" he brought his hands in front of him and blew them apart while making an explosion sound.

"Yeah." I reached up and touched the cold glass, focusing on the raindrops as they came together and created tiny rivers of water.

Bailer sighed heavily. "It's the nurse, isn't it?" He stepped back and started pacing. "It's always the nurse—the Nightingale Effect I think they call it."

I turned from the window, wearing a bemused expression. "That's for soldiers who fall in love with their caretakers. Not for the grandson of a lady who fell and broke her hip."

"Same thing." He threw up a hand. "I can't take you on set like this—depression bleeds on screen and heartbreaks are horrible for careers."

I scrubbed my face. "What do you want me to do?"

He stopped pacing and considered me from head to toe. His shoulders fell and he heaved a great sigh. "Bring her here."

"What?" That was the last thing I expected him to say. "What about Jackie and our perfect on-and-off screen romance?" The words were laced with sarcasm. The relationship was as much his idea as Jackie's agent's. They'd been so proud, and it all felt seamless, though I knew they worked hard to control our image as a couple in the media.

He shook his head. "I have no idea. I'll figure it out."

I stared at him in open-mouthed shock.

"Look, I'm not going to sugarcoat it. You'll take a hit. Knowing Jackie's agent, she'll make sure you pay—publicly."

"I don't care." I said the words without thinking. The moment they were out, the truth of them filled me up more than the giant burrito I'd eaten yesterday. Penny—and Katie—were more important than the next role. They were more precious than any award I'd won or could win in the future. If I could spend the rest of my life snuggling them on the couch and watching princess movies, I'd be the happiest and luckiest man alive.

Hollywood had lost its luster. I couldn't chase after the glitz and glam like a cat after a laser. Not when I could have the woman of my dreams in my arms—not when the family I'd longed for all my life was within reach.

My hopes were suddenly dashed like the waves against the shore outside.

"I left her. I left town with Jackie and you." I gestured toward him. "And I left behind the threat of a paternity suit and her broken heart." I dug my fingers into my hair. "Oh man! I so messed up."

Bailer punched me in the arm. "Then go back. Airplanes fly both ways you know."

I dropped my arms to my side. "It won't be easy."

He lifted a shoulder. "So beg for another chance."

"She can be stubborn."

"You can be charming." He pulled out his phone and started typing.

"What are you doing?"

"Booking you an early flight. It leaves in less than six hours. Pack."

I headed for my room. Bailer followed on my heels.

"You have my back, right?" I asked.

"Of course." He didn't look up as he inputted my driver's license information.

"Then you can tell Jackie."

He scowled.

I smiled. "This is why I pay you the big bucks." I smacked him on the back. "And I don't know when or if I'm coming back, so…"

He sighed again. "Just keep me posted. I can work a lot of magic, but I can't spin gold, so let's keep the conversation open."

I nodded. I wasn't going to make any decisions until I had a chance to talk to Penny anyway. For all I knew, she'd kick me out on my rear and tell me to talk to her lawyer. But, if she cared about me at all, if she'd give me a chance to bring us together, I'd do everything in my power—move heaven and earth if I had to—to finally make our family whole.

I checked my watch. Less than six hours. I could hardly wait.

19

PENNY

I stood on the front stoop, trying to control Katie, who'd forgone a nap and was now spinning out of control on the porch. We were waiting for our ride to the airport, and I was already a jumble of nerves. Katie's whining and agitation weren't helping me either.

I knew it was because she could feel my anxiety over this whole situation, so I was trying to cut her some slack, but it was a struggle.

Mom had insisted that she call a ride service for me. I was trying hard not to feel annoyed that she didn't want to drive her daughter to the airport, but it was tough. Mom just shook her head and said I wouldn't regret getting a ride, so I took that as my cue to drop the subject.

My heart picked up speed as I blew out a sigh of relief when I saw a red Chevy truck pull into the driveway. I didn't care who was driving as long as I could belt my daughter in the back seat and give myself a few moments of peace—until I realized Tag was behind the wheel and Brit's shining smile was flashing at me from the front seat.

Tears sprang to my eyes as I hurried to open the passenger door. Brit beat me to it, and a moment later, we were high school best friends again, squealing and hugging as we jumped up and down.

"You're home!" I said through my tears.

Brit laughed. "And you're engaged to my fiancé?"

Heat permeated my cheeks as my lie flashed in my mind. "Right. About that..." I gave her my big puppy eyes and saddest face, hoping she'd forgive me. "Chris was back, and I was a mess. What was I supposed to do?"

Brit studied me and then nodded. "Makes sense." She wrapped her arm around my shoulders and escorted me to the back seat of the cab. Tag had already belted Katie in and set our suitcases in the bed. When Katie saw Brit, she squealed and kicked her feet. Brit leaned over the seat to kiss both her cheeks.

I climbed in and buckled up, and a few moments later, we were on the road. Katie had settled down. With her favorite blanket and Elsa doll—plus the gentle pressure from her seatbelt—she was moments away from falling asleep. We had an hour ride to the airport, and if she decided to zonk out, I wasn't going to stop her.

I filled the time talking to Brit. She was home for a week for her grandpa's funeral. Plus, she needed to tie up some loose ends for the wedding in two months. I told her to make a list, and that I would be happy to help her where I could.

She then turned the conversation to me, forcing me to recount the entire Chris experience. I didn't hold anything back as I talked it over with her. Even when I got to the kiss, and Tag made gagging sounds from the driver's seat. We both socked him in the arm, and he raised his hands, swearing he'd be just a listener from that moment on.

By the time we pulled into the airport parking lot, Brit was bouncing up and down in her seat. "So you're going to tell him that you love him?"

I paused with my hand on the door handle. Hearing those words out loud seemed to halt my brain function. I peeked over at her, not able to fight the smile that emerged. "I'm going to try."

Her smile widened. "I'm so happy for you, Pen. You've been living with this pain for far too long. I'm glad to see that everything is out in the open."

I climbed out of the truck and waited as Tag unbuckled Katie and handed her over to me. Katie could sleep like a log when she wanted to, and right now was one of those moments. Her head rested on my shoulder, making it impossible for me to carry anything else.

What I had wanted to be a movie-like reunion seemed to be failing. With a sleepy four-year-old, expectations had to be lowered.

Brit and Tag walked alongside me as we entered the airport. They were carrying our luggage and car seat. I was grateful for my friends and their willingness to not only forgive me but support me. A wave of emotion washed over me when I recounted all the people in my life who had helped me through everything.

I was a truly blessed person.

Once Katie and I were checked in and our luggage was collected, I gave a side hug to Tag and Brit and promised to be back as soon as I saw Chris. With Brit being home, I wanted to see her as much as I could.

Brit waved off my promise and told me to take all the time I needed to fix my little family. She'd be back in a few months and had no intention of leaving for a long time after that. I gave her another quick side hug, shouldered my purse and Katie's backpack, and hurried to the security point check-in.

It didn't take long to get through the line. I was already pre-screened, so it made the process much smoother. They even allowed me to carry Katie through the body scanner, which was nice, waking Katie now would only mean torture for those around us.

When I finally got to the gate, I collapsed in a chair and stuck my feet out in front of me. I blew out my breath as I tipped my face back and closed my eyes. We were on our way. I was hours away from landing in California to look for Chris in a state of millions. I wasn't sure if I was crazy or not, but I had to try.

Ten minutes later—after a short but much needed catnap for me—Katie began to wiggle and eventually slid onto the floor. Her eyes were bloodshot, but her normally cheerful demeanor was back. She blinked a few times as she glanced around.

"Where awe we, Mommy?" she asked as she spun slowly in a circle.

"We're at the airport," I said, straightening and adjusting our bags so they were no longer skiwampus next to me.

"Wow," she whispered.

I'd never taken her on a plane before, so watching her amazement as she glanced around made my heart squeeze. I loved this little girl more than life itself. The thought of Chris and me making a run at being a family made me happier than I'd been in a long time.

"Remember Chris?" I asked as I reached out and smoothed down her hair. I'd put it into braids this morning, but with her earlier agitation, she'd shaken some strands loose.

Katie's expression turned contemplative as she nodded. "He make gwood tea."

I smiled. "We're on our way to see him."

Katie crawled up onto my lap. "Why?"

I sucked in my breath and held it for a moment. I hated that I had lied for so long. That I thought the truth was more painful than keeping it secret.

"Well, he's your daddy."

Katie turned to meet my gaze. She held it for a moment and then nodded as she pressed her hands onto my cheeks. "I know."

I blinked. "You know?"

She nodded again. "I know. I picked him. I told Elsa I wanted a daddy, and then Chris came." She smiled over at me.

"So you're okay with this?"

Katie sighed and slipped off my lap again, seeming to have already grown bored with our conversation. To me, this was an earth-shattering truth. To her, it was an answer to a wish. Watching my daughter take my mistake in stride made me sad. I didn't deserve this second chance I was getting.

"Daddy!" Katie exclaimed.

I glanced over at her to see her standing close to the walkway, staring off at something in the distance. "Katie, no. Daddy's not here —" But before I could stop her, she took off.

Panic rose up inside of me as I grabbed our bags and hurried after her. She was weaving and dodging through busy travelers as they tried to avoid running her over. I called after her as I apologized to the people I'd almost toppled over.

By the time the crowd thinned, I found her standing next to a man who was crouched down talking to her. Fear that she was talking to a stranger choked me. I hurried over and grabbed Katie. "Excuse me, what do you think—"

All thought left my mind as I was met with Chris's luscious brown eyes. He straightened and raised his eyebrows as he swept his gaze over me. My entire body flushed with heat under his stare.

"Where...Why...?" The questions inside of me were competing to come out all at once, and I couldn't find the brainpower to force the right one to the top.

"Where are you guys going?" he asked.

Before I could answer, a woman walked by and muttered something under her breath about rude people standing in the walkway. Thankfully, Chris took charge. He reached out, pressed his hand onto my lower back, and guided me over to the small playground that had been set up in the airport.

Katie wiggled and wiggled until I let her down, and then she gleefully ran over to the slide. Now, alone with Chris, I felt vulnerable. I wrapped my arms around my chest as I took in a deep breath.

"You told her about me?" he asked. His voice was low and filled with emotion.

I peeked over at him to see him studying me. "Yes," I whispered.

He nodded. "It was strange, hearing her call out *Daddy*." Then he blew out his breath. "But I liked it."

"She seemed to take the news in stride. Said she'd wished for you." Tears stung my eyes as my mistakes rose to the forefront of my mind. "I'm so sorry. We were heading to California to tell you this."

Chris's jaw muscles flinched as he stared off in Katie's direction. I could tell he was keeping track of her movements. A dad for a few short days and already he looked like a pro.

"I understand why you did it, even if I don't agree with it." He peeked over at me. "I'm a good guy, and I'll be a great dad."

I swallowed. "I know."

He stepped closer to me, his forearm brushing mine. "I'd make an even better husband."

My heart began to pound as I stood there, staring at him. Was he talking about me? Did I dare hope? "I'm sure you would. Jackie's a lucky woman."

Chris paused and then sighed. "Jackie was a publicity stunt. She's not my person." He turned and wrapped both hands around my upper arms. He dipped down slightly to catch my gaze. "You're my person. You've *always* been my person."

Everything seemed to fade around me as I stared into Chris's eyes. They were deep and longing and all that I'd been missing in my life.

"Can you forgive me?" Sure, he loved me because I was Katie's mom, but could he get over the fact that I'd lied to him?

He furrowed his brow. "Promise to never hide any of our future children from me?"

My heart took off galloping at his words. *Future children?* That thought made me feel warm and whole. The kind of love that was coursing through me had been one that I'd convinced myself I no longer needed.

"I promise."

He held my gaze before glancing in Katie's direction and then back to me. "Then, yes, I can forgive you."

Before I could stop myself, I rose up onto my tiptoes and pressed my lips to his. It was a soft and questioning kiss. As if I wanted to make sure it was okay.

His hands found my waist and pulled me in as he deepened the kiss. My entire body melted into his embrace as he held me. Every part of me fit perfectly against every part of him. We were born to fall in love. I was sure, somewhere, it was written in the stars that we were meant to be together.

A strong tug on my shirt drew me out of our kiss. I pulled back and glanced down to see Katie staring up at us. "Are you gonna get mawied?" she asked.

Chris chuckled as he bent down to her level. "What do you think? Should we get married?"

Katie glanced up at me and then back to Chris. "Yeah," she said before she turned and ran back to the playground.

Chris straightened and pulled me over to him. Standing behind me, he wrapped his arms around me and pulled me against him. "We're at the airport and I have no ring, but I can't help but ask you something I should have asked a long time ago."

I sighed as I leaned into him. All the broken pieces of my past seemed to be falling away, and the only thing I could focus on was the hope of my future. "What's that?"

He nuzzled my neck for a moment and then whispered the sweetest two words I'd ever heard.

"Marry me?"

EPILOGUE

MASON

I tugged at my collar, grateful that it was Jaxon and Lottie mingling and accepting congratulations on their engagement and not me. They were all smiles and doe-eyed looks for one another, so it didn't seem to bother them too much. Lottie normally had a hard time in the spotlight, so I kept an eye out for her.

I also had an eye on the perimeter and the exits. Security was a job hazard.

Penny and Chris sat at a round table playing a game of checkers with Katie. Chris had taught her how to play, and she was hooked. They looked like a happy little family, Penny's giant rock of a ring glinting in the light. They were planning on a wedding next year—to keep the focus on Lottie this year. I envied them—no matter that the road to this moment had been pockmarked, twisted, and uphill the whole way.

I'd never really gotten out of the habit of checking my surroundings after being discharged. The Army pounded survival techniques into my skull, and I had no intention of letting them go. I was all too aware of what one moment of relaxation could cost me.

I circled the room, checking on things for Mom as I went. Lottie was usually her second-in-command—when she wasn't the guest of honor. I'd been recruited to make sure the buffet tables stayed full. She'd hired a full staff, wanting to spend every minute celebrating her daughter's engagement.

I turned in time to see one of the male servers put a spoon in his pocket. My head jerked back in surprise. It wasn't like the flatware was expensive, but there was no reason to allow theft to take place. Especially right under my nose.

That would not only be a personal insult but a professional one.

I stomped his direction, my eyes focused on him and him alone as he made his way inside the house. The servers were all dressed the same and he blended in with the crowd. I lost sight of him for two seconds. Surging forward, I shoved myself between two men, muttering, "excuse me," as I did so.

One of them grunted. I looked over my shoulder to offer an apology and my hand hit a tray, sending hors d'oeuvres crashing to the ground.

"I'm so sorry." I caught sight of the thief and was ready to chase after him when I heard a familiar voice say, "Wouldn't expect anything else."

The icy tone in the otherwise melodic sound stopped me in my tracks. I turned slowly, giving my full attention to the server who was crouched down, picking up jumbo shrimp. "Sadie?"

She didn't look at me. "Yeah."

I crouched next to her, my ears burning with embarrassment and shame, the thief forgotten. My reaction to her wasn't new. I pressed through it—as I had a thousand times before and as I would for forever.

My best friend's widow was my responsibility—no matter what she said. And I'd live and breathe to make her life easier, better, happier—if she'd let me.

"Let me get those." I picked up the only shrimp near me and set it on the tray balanced on her left hand.

She sighed. "You're too late." Her eyes narrowed, adding the words she was thinking but didn't throw in my face. *Just like always.*

I reached for her elbow to help her stand, but she evaded my touch.

"We must be getting along better—you didn't tell me to leave," I joked. Anything to tease out her smile.

She glanced around. "I can't tell you to leave your own house, now can I?"

"I don't live here." I had a house two doors down from her, and she knew it. No doubt she wanted me to move back in here just so I'd be farther away from her. Well, that wasn't going to happen. I made a vow to my buddy before he died, and I planned to keep it.

"Well, it's not my party." She headed for the kitchen, dumping the tray's contents in a garbage as she passed.

I looked down at the heap of pathetic, beaten shrimp—a shadow of the beautiful display they'd been when they left the kitchen. Sadie was like that. She'd been so beautiful. So vibrant. Then Parker didn't come home, and she was…well, she wasn't garbage.

I huffed. I'm an idiot. I'm ruminating over the garbage can. The things that woman caused me to do…

And like the idiot I was, I followed her out the door. She had a new tray in her hand, this one with mushroom buttons. They smelled so good my stomach rumbled. "Hey," I called after her.

She ignored me and offered her tray to the first person standing outside the kitchen. When Mayor Thomas shook his head, she pressed on, her smile as frozen as the ice sculpture near the pool.

"Can I have one of those?" I demanded. I regretted my tone instantly.

She turned and held the tray as far away from her as possible. I let my hand hover over the selection, as if I were trying to pick the best one, but I was looking at her. "How are you doing?"

Her shoulders dropped. "Fine. The insurance kicked in—finally—and paid for the Taurus."

Her car had caught fire in an accident, and I'd pulled her son from the flaming vehicle. I was lucky I came upon them that night. Blessed beyond measure that I didn't have any flashbacks to deal with—the

HIS SECRET BABY

flames and her screams easily could have triggered something. But they didn't and we made it out alive, both of us.

I'd taken one look at her owl-big eyes and thrown myself into the passenger side of the car, not caring if it blew up while I was in there. I couldn't let her lose her son. Not after…

"Would you like me to go car shopping with you? I can take you over there so you can drive your new car off the lot."

She rolled her eyes. "The insurance didn't give me that much money, Sheriff *McKnight*. I'll be shopping the classifieds."

"Hey, none of this is mine." I waved my hands around indicating the pool, the white tent, the serving staff, and the mounds of food. "Okay? I'm not some little rich kid. I work every day for what I have."

She held up a tray and smiled sweetly. "More mushrooms?"

I shook my head. "No thanks." She pushed my buttons until I pushed back. This was how our conversations always went, so it shouldn't have been a surprise. For a moment, my walls thinned, and I looked at her, really looked. The woman I saw used to be my friend. "I lost a friend. I don't want to lose another."

She stiffened and sucked air in through her nose. Her eyes widened, and she stepped back. "We were never friends. Parker was your friend, not me." She sighed. "I'm at work. Please don't talk to me again." She fled like a rabbit who was late for an important date.

I ran my hand down my face. I really needed to stop letting Katie pick our movies. I was beginning to narrate my life like I lived in one of them.

My gaze bored into the crowd of people Sadie had slipped through when she made her getaway. I prayed that she'd cut through them again. I prayed that she'd come back to talk to me. According to her mom, she hadn't talked about losing Parker at all. She'd just bottled it up inside. It fizzed in there, like shaking a can of soda. One of these days, the top was going to blow clean off.

If I could just get her to…

I sighed.

I may have been a sergeant and the town sheriff, but saving Sadie was the toughest job of my life.

ABOUT THE AUTHOR

ANNE-MARIE MEYER

Anne-Marie Meyer lives south of the Twin Cities in MN. She spends her days with her knight in shining armor, four princes, and a baby princess.

When she's not running after her kids, she's dreaming up romantic stories. She loves to take her favorite moments in the books and movies she loves and tries to figure out a way to make them new and fresh.

Join her newsletter at anne-mariemeyer.com

ABOUT THE AUTHOR

LUCY MCCONNELL

Lucy McConnell loves romance, chocolate, Christmas and Elvis.

Her short fiction has been published in *Women's World Magazine*, and she has written for *Parents' Magazine* and *The Deseret News*.

When she's not writing, you can find Lucy volunteering at the elementary school or church, shuttling kids to basketball or rodeos, skiing with her family or curled up with a good book.

You can sign up for her newsletter—and get a **free book**—at https://mybookcave.com/d/290d4f96/

You can find more of her romances here: https://www.amazon.com/Lucy-McConnell/e/B00GKS2ZC2?ref=sr_ntt_srch_lnk_3&qid=1580951756&sr=1-3

Or visit her website at:

AuthorLucyMcConnell.com

Printed in Great Britain
by Amazon